Top Secret: Escape from Iran

G. Gray Garland

AuthorHouse™
1663 Liberty Drive, Suite 200
Bloomington, IN 47403
www.authorhouse.com
Phone: 1-800-839-8640

© 2009 G. Gray Garland. All rights reserved.

No part of this book may be reproduced, stored in a retrieval system, or
transmitted by any means without the written permission of the author.

First published by AuthorHouse 2/3/2009

ISBN: 978-1-4389-3358-0 (e)
ISBN: 978-1-4389-3359-7 (sc)
ISBN: 978-1-4389-3360-3 (hc)

Library of Congress Control Number: 2008910711

Printed in the United States of America
Bloomington, Indiana

This book is printed on acid-free paper.

This is a work of fiction. Plot and characters are purely a product of the author's

imagination. Any resemblance to actual persons, living or dead, businesses, companies,

events or locales is entirely coincidental.

Front of the cover was designed by Cody Whitby

This book is dedicated to my brother, the author, Landon W. Garland, without whose encouragement it would never have been completed.

CHAPTER 1

THE WHITE HOUSE ,WASHINGTON, D.C.

EARLY NOVEMBER

You could hear a pin drop.

The Cabinet Room was so silent that those in attendance almost feared to breathe.

No one had seen the president so upset. He slammed his hand down on the table so hard that several items in front of him bounced up. He stared at the Director of the CIA for what seemed like an eternity. "You don't know! You don't know!," he almost screamed. "Every time I ask you. I get the same damn answer. "I don't know. I don't know. I have nothing new to report on Iran."

"We've got to find out what's going on in Iran. We've got a problems in Afghanistan, we've got problems in Iraq, and there is North Korea. We don't seem to know what the hell is going on anywhere, especially Iran."

The president continued with sarcasm, "Why can't our vaunted intelligence agencies find anything out."

Dead silence. No one dared to speak. Finally someone mumbled, "Remember Howard Stafford?" Most of those in attendance remembered. Howard Stafford had attempted to argue with an angry President. He had disappeared from the Cabinet meetings. He was probably now stamping passports in Zimbabwe.

Finally George Amaturo, one of the anonymous assistants lining the back wall, "Mr. President, you dropped your fountain pen."

"No, it's not mine," handing it back to Amaturo.

"It's mine," said Secretary of State, Alexander Hatfield. "It must have bounced off the table."

This drew a laugh from everyone, including the President.

The ice was broken, at least for now.

CHAPTER 2

THE WHITEHOUSE

FAMILY QUARTERS TWO DAYS LATER

The President of the United States of America was still angry, very angry. And it was really not his fault. He slammed the paper he was reading onto his desk. The newspapers, as usual, were giving him a very hard time because of what they called the Administration's "intelligence failures with respect to Iran."

Although it was not yet seven o'clock in the morning, the President, usually an early riser, was still in his pajamas and wearing a blue bathrobe with a large Presidential Seal affixed to it. He was in his study in the living quarters, drinking coffee and fuming over the newspapers when a Secret Service Agent showed the Director of The Central Intelligence Agency into the small study.

The Director, who had never been in this room, noticed the maroon walls were covered with family photographs. On the top of the President's desk were the morning editions of the Washington newspapers and The New York Times. They looked as if they had already been read. They had.

The President got up from his chair. "Morning! Coffee, Jay, Jay? Black as usual?"

"Yes, please."

The President, trying to hold back his anger, poured coffee from a silver coffee urn on the antique credenza behind his desk into a delicate china cup and handed the cup with saucer to the Director.

"Before we start, tell me what you have found for me on Iran."

When the Director answered, "Nothing new, I'm afraid."

The normally calm and controlled demeanor of the President of the United States turned to red-faced anger as he stood and slammed his fist down on his desk, so hard, that several items on his desk bounced into the air.

He stared coldly at the Director of the Central Intelligence Agency for a long moment and then erupted. "Jay Jay, if your team can't get this done with all the money we're pouring into the CIA, I'll get someone else to run it. I'm damned sick and tired of waiting to get an answer about Iran from you. It's now a political issue. Have you read the morning papers?"

When the Director had finished his morning briefing, the President was still angry and again chewed him out, but good.

Escape from Iran

The President must have pressed a button. The door immediately opened, and a Secret Service Agent ushered the Director out of the room. The meeting was over.

The President had repeatedly asked the Director of the Central Intelligence Agency, John Jacob Winthrop Cabot, IV, about lack of intelligence on Iran. Even Cabot could not understand why the CIA was progressing so slowly in obtaining any information about Iran's aiding terrorists and building weapons of mass destruction, and when the President had inquired Cabot had always replied, "We're working hard on it."

Today this was definitely not the answer the President wanted to hear. Cabot felt very frustrated. He had worked hard on this without any real success. *I have done everything humanly possible. This is unfair. The president just doesn't know the facts.*

The weather did not lift the sagging spirits of Director Cabot, as he exited the White House. In November Washington can be cold, and dreary with the feel of the coming winter in the air. Today was no exception. Outside it was thirty-eight degrees with a cold rain. To the Director it felt even colder. He shuddered as he waited for his car to pull up. The President's anger was just another straw on the camel's back, a big straw, however. The day had started with a downer. He had told his wife at breakfast that they would have to cancel their planned winter vacation to their rented house in the Barbados because of his workload. That had led to a heated argument about why he had to work so hard. She ranted and raved. She did not understand him anymore. He really did not need the job or the money. His job took so much of his time that he no longer had any time for his family. He had left his house in Georgetown in a very depressed mood. Getting chewed out by the President only added to his depression.

The Director's black Mercury Marquis sedan, nondescript except for the cluster of antennas on its trunk, passed out of the White House gate, its windshield wipers swishing back and forth to clear the rain. As it exited the gate it was followed by a large black Chevrolet Suburban station wagon, also with numerous antennas on its roof. The Chevrolet Suburban contained Cabot's security detail. Cabot was riding in the front seat of the Mercury where he liked to ride. Riding in the front seat with his driver made him feel like one of the boys. Jerry Madigan, his driver and his personal bodyguard, who was an ex-Marine Sergeant in the Marine Raiders, probably had a different opinion on this.

Cabot was a tall, slender man with a full head of graying hair. To many he appeared to be a somewhat arrogant and demanding person. Others, who knew him well, said underneath it all he was just shy. He was the eldest son of a politically prominent and wealthy Boston Brahmin family. He had attended Yale and Harvard Business School and had made his mark and lots of money on Wall Street. He purchased most of his clothes in London from a Saville Row tailor. Some thought

Escape from Iran

he had also bought his job as Director of the CIA with the large donations he and his family made to the Republican Party.

Cabot picked up a microphone, one of several on the dashboard, and thumbed the key. The answer was instantaneous. "I'm on my way back. I should be there in about thirty minutes. I want Sampson and Hogan waiting in my conference room when I get there."

Behind their backs both had nicknames. John Sampson, the Deputy Director, a short balding man with thick glasses and ill fitting, rumpled suits, was known behind his back as "Jay Two", and Mike Hogan, the Director of Covert Operations, known mostly because of his tough approach to business as "Iron Mike" or sometimes because of his large physique as "The Hulk" after the wrestler Hulk Hogan.

Without waiting for a reply, he returned the microphone to its holder and said to the driver, "Jerry, if we run into any traffic, use the siren and lights. I'm in a hurry."

As they approached the Memorial Bridge to Virginia, the traffic became heavier. The driver picked up another microphone from the dashboard, "Spyglass" to "Big Foot", stay close. We're moving out."

The flashing lights and sirens on both cars came alive, and the two vehicles moved rapidly, weaving through the heavy morning commuter traffic. Twenty-five minutes later Cabot strolled into the director's conference room at CIA headquarters in Langley, Virginia. The room was a large, somewhat narrow, room, painted government gray with nothing on the walls except several covered screens and a projector. There were several easels placed around the room with covers over them to hide what might be on them.

Waiting for him there at a long conference table were Sampson and Hogan. Without so much as a word to either one, Cabot immediately sat down at one end of the table.

Sampson, noting Cabot seemed upset, stood up and went to a sideboard where there was an electric coffee pot, coffee mugs and a plate of doughnuts. He poured steaming coffee into a white mug with the CIA shield on it and handed it to Cabot. "John, you look like you need this. I take it your meeting with the President did not go well."

Without answering, Cabot shrugged, sat down and took a large sip. He put his coffee cup on the conference table, "I asked you to meet me to discuss Iran. The Iran situation is becoming extremely tense, and I'm beginning to take a lot of heat from the White House. Every time I brief the President he asks me what we have found out for him about Iran. This time he really chewed me up one side and down the other because we don't have any hard information on what they're doing. Obviously we do know from various sources that they are buying or attempting to buy vast quantities of chemicals and other materials, which we believe are being used to make biological and nuclear weapons, but for all of our efforts we have no hard information beyond this. This morning

Escape from Iran

when I briefed the President, he stated in no uncertain terms that we must find out what is going on in Iran.

The President said this is of the utmost importance, and that no stone should be left unturned. From what we know from our satellite coverage and from what other sources tell us, we have learned quite a lot about what the Iranians are doing. We are absolutely convinced that they are developing biological and nuclear weapons. The President says we must have hard evidence to convince the world that what we claim is true. Without this evidence he thinks we are virtually unable to take any action to protect our national security. I am afraid I have to agree with this."

Sampson, who appeared to be listening intently, paused, and took off his glasses. He proceeded to clean them with a handkerchief, returned the glasses to his nose and he replied, "What we really need is to get hold of a couple of their top scientists. They could give us evidence of what the Iranians are doing and why they are purchasing so much suspicious stuff."

Cabot, already on edge from his visit to the White House, was now very irritated by Sampson's pause to clean his eyeglasses. He thought, *"Why does that bastard always pause to clean his glasses before he answers a question? Does he think that makes him look wise or does he need time to think?"*

The Director responded very sarcastically to Sampson, "That's very obvious, but how are we going to do this? You don't even really know who most of the scientists are, much less how to contact any of them. The Iranians have kept a close lid on those people. They're scared to death of talking to any outsider. We cannot even get near them."

Hogan, looked at Cabot and thought, *"The pressure is really getting to him."* Hogan, a 6 foot 2 inch, 230 pound former football star at the University of Denver, had been recruited by the CIA while he was still in college. He wanted to play football for the NFL, but he had been turned down by the NFL because of a knee injury. He had then accepted a position with the CIA. He was fearless, and nothing seemed to bother him. Hogan always appeared very comfortable in handling his job as head of covert operations.

He spoke up, "Yeah, that's true, but we do know that one of the main purchasing agents for the bastards is Robert McClelland, an American citizen living in Iran. McClelland probably knows what they are planning to manufacture and he probably knows all of the major scientists working on these projects, because he is one of their primary purchasing agents for this material. If we could somehow get next to McClelland and have him work with us, he could give us a lot of information and maybe even persuade one or more of the scientists to come over to us."

Escape from Iran

Cabot, who had been slouched in his chair straightened up. He was now very interested. He inquired, "Who is this McClelland?"

"Just a minute." Hogan put down his coffee cup, picked up a nearby phone, and pressed an intercom button, "Sarah, send me the file on Robert McClelland. It's in the top drawer of my desk."

Within minutes a uniformed messenger knocked on the door and delivered the requested file folder. Hogan signed for it, and the messenger left the room.

Hogan opened the red folder that was marked "Top Secret" in bold, black letters. He removed several sheets of paper and read, "Robert Baxter McClelland, white male, born January 12, 1967, at Lexington, Kentucky. Graduated from Thomas Jefferson High School in 1984 with better than average grades."

The Director, nervously drumming the table with his fingers, abruptly interrupted Hogan, "Skip the background, and tell us how he got to what he's doing now."

Hogan, somewhat taken aback by the Director's almost angry tone of voice, started to read again from the file, "McClelland went to Iran during the Shah's regime as a chief engineer for Baker, Kean and Coleman Company, a global engineering and construction company, headquartered in Tulsa, Oklahoma. Baker, Kean was at that time involved in hundreds of millions of dollars of construction for the Iranian Government, erecting power plants, and constructing oil

G. Gray Garland

refineries, bridges, highways, airports and highways, etc. While in Iran McClelland became very friendly with a number of those who were the government purchasing agents, and he was able to purchase a number of hard to acquire items for them. He later branched out on his own and started to acquire and sell hard to get items to the government of the Shah. After the Shah was deposed, he continued to live in Iran and to do business with the new regime, many members of whom he already knew well, and who continued in their former jobs. He was undoubtedly permitted to continue his business because of his ability to obtain those items that were difficult for the new regime to purchase, mainly because their export was banned by the United States. The Iranians were always somewhat suspicious of McClelland, but after some time they accepted him as a sort of ally. He has apparently made a very large fortune of several hundred million dollars in this business and lives like royalty with several magnificent homes, cars, and airplanes, including a new $30 million Gulfstream executive jet, which was purchased by him using a front corporation, AirMac, GBH, based in Switzerland."

Cabot again interrupted with sarcasm, "But McClelland is a traitor. He does'nt want any part of us. He's not going to talk to us"

Sampson ignored Cabot's remark and interjected, "Regardless of that, he would be very valuable to us. There must be some way that we can turn him."

Escape from Iran

Cabot shrugged as if to say "So what!" "I don't see how."

Hogan replied, "We have tried several times to contact him, each time without success. He has become a very wealthy man dealing with the Iranians. He doesn't trust anyone we might have contact him. Besides, if he were to return to the United States, he would worry about being tried as a traitor. There just isn't any real incentive for him to help us. I'm not certain that he is not afraid for his life. Even if he were to come back to the United States, you know the Iranians, they would not hesitate to assassinate him, if they had any inkling he might be working with us."

Cabot, now somewhat calmed down, said, "Why not try again to contact him? We don't have any other plan on the table." and continued, "What do you know about his habits? Is he married?"

Hogan replied, "As far as we know he has never married. We do know this. He is not gay. He does like women. He often invites them from Europe, but never, as far as we know, from the United States. He seldom leaves Iran. He does most of his business by telephone and fax from his offices and homes there. He usually makes one or two trips a year to Paris or Switzerland, sometimes to Spain, but he is always surrounded by bodyguards, who do not let anyone near him. Undoubtedly these bodyguards are really not so much for his protection, but to make sure he doesn't stray."

"Well, what do you suggest?" the Director asked.

G. Gray Garland

"I don't know," Hogan replied. Closely watching the Director, he continued, "I think with all the pressure the President is putting on this, perhaps he could arrange with the Attorney General to offer McClelland immunity from any prosecution. Then we might have a chance of turning him. He has all the money he'd ever want. It's probably somewhat lonely for him as a foreigner living in Iran. If only there was some way we could talk with him, we might have a chance. However, we do not have anyone in Iran that we know who can contact McClelland. Hogan continued, closely watching the Director, "We have tried a number of times to contact McClelland without exposing our hand. For example, knowing that McClelland liked pretty women, we had one of our female agents attempt to approach him at a concert. He was standing in the lobby of the concert hall. He had just finished a conversation with one of his Iranian friends and was starting up the stairs to his box. Before our agent could begin a conversation with McClelland, his bodyguards blocked her access, and McClelland continued on apparently without noticing her."

Cabot again with sarcasm, "Don't we have anyone in Iran who knows anything? Can't we find out what McClelland does in Iran when he leaves his home or office?"

Sampson, "What good will that do? What about any of the scientists? Don't we know any of them?"

Escape from Iran

Hogan, stopped playing with his coffee cup and closed the file folder. "As I said, we don't know any of the scientists well enough to contact them. In any event, they are all afraid to talk with anyone. They are afraid for their lives. We don't have anyone in our organization that McClelland would trust. We do have an agent there who might be able to follow McClelland to some extent. How beneficial that will be, I don't know. What we need to do is to recruit someone that McClelland would trust, one of his old friends.

How do we do this? We go back through McClelland's life and determine who his friends were. We then see if we can get one of them to work with us in getting next to McClelland. It may take some time, but in my opinion that's probably the only way for us to go."

Director Cabot stopped sipping his coffee, "At least that is a positive idea. See what you can do Mike, and report back to me with what you have no later than next Friday. This is top priority"

"Yes, Sir."

The meeting adjourned.

CHAPTER 3

THE FOLLOWING FRIDAY

It was early in the morning in the Director's Conference Room at CIA headquarters in Langley, Virginia. It was still dark and grey outside. The bright, fluorescent lights were a little bothersome so early in the day.

Sampson and Hogan sat silently across from each other at the end of the large conference table, drinking coffee and waiting for Cabot, each of them wondering about Cabot's mood and trying not to look uneasy. The Director had scheduled the meeting for 7:00 am. It was already 7:30 am, and Cabot, who was noted for being prompt, was not there.

At last the double doors of Cabot's adjacent office opened, and he walked briskly into the conference room. Without so much as a "Good Morning" or "Sorry I'm late," he pulled his chair out from his end of the tablesat down and said, "Well, Mike, what do you have?"

Escape from Iran

Hogan leafing through a file folder and trying to look relaxed answered, "We're still looking at this, but we do have quite a bit of information. Did you know that McClelland's father once worked for us?"

Cabot and Sampson both look very surprised. Sampson said, "No. Why didn't we know this?"

Cabot with sarcasm in his voice, "Just like a lot of things around here that we don't know. I don't know how helpful that momentous bit of information will be. Mike, what else do you know?"

Hogan was unfazed and continued, "McClelland went to Virginia Military Institute and was later in the Marines. As best we can tell he had a number of close friends both at VMI and in the Marines. I have a list of some of them here. We can see if any of them are worth recruiting for this project."

Cabot, interrupting, asked, "Do you have a copy of the list?"

Hogan opened the file folder in front of him." Yes, I have extra copies for you here." Hogan then distributed copies to Cabot and Sampson.

Cabot took several minutes to review the list before responding, "We really only have three or four names here worth looking at. Tony Brown is dead. We obviously can't use him. Elmon Harrison is a United States Senator. I don't think we can use him. Hugh Nesby does not appear to get along with or be able to keep a job with anyone for very long. He's had about a half a dozen jobs since he graduated from college, and no one who was interviewed said anything good about him. That leaves Raymond Gates and Alex Blair."

Cabot, continuing to study his file folder, spoke up. "Gates appears to be in poor health and would have no reason to contact McClelland, but Blair might possibly have a good excuse to go to Europe where he might accidentally run into McClelland. I see Blair was in the Marines with McClelland after they graduated in the same class from VMI. It does not say what they did. It looks like it might be something secret. You know the Marines though. They'll give us nothing. I also notice Blair owns a number of businesses including a metals business. He is a major owner of Mercer Metals, a company that makes some of the metals that the Iranians have been trying to buy. In fact, Mercer Metals makes many of the metals that go into our nuclear missiles. The Iranians might really like this. If we handle this right, McClelland may take the hook. Maybe then we can get the camel's nose into the tent."

Standing up to get a cup of coffee from the sideboard, Cabot turned and directed Hogan, "Read what you have on Blair."

Hogan flipped through the report and continued. "I have something interesting here." He paused to take a sip of his coffee. "I had the FBI do a quick check on Blair. Here is what they came back with. Alex Blair is a six foot, white male, thirty-eight years old, probably weighs between 180 and 190 pounds. He is an attorney and a businessman,

Escape from Iran

married with three children - two boys and a girl. He lives in a large residence at 200 Northumberland Heights, seven miles west of Richmond, Virginia. The property is in an exclusive area, overlooking the James River. He also has a farm in Ligonier, Pennsylvania, which is approximately fifty-five miles east of Pittsburgh, Pennsylvania. Eight neighbors in Richmond were interviewed, no negative comments.

"He grew up in Richmond, Virginia, attended St. Christopher's Preparatory School, Virginia Military Institute, and the University of Virginia Law School and Harvard Business School - -"

Sampson interrupted, clearing his throat, paused for a moment and looked at Cabot. He liked to bait him. "Another "B-Schooler." Did you know him?"

Cabot, trying not to show his annoyance, replied, "No, he was after my time."

Hogan then continued. "We did not have time to obtain any school records. He did graduate from all of the schools. Several persons interviewed said he was very intelligent. With all the money he has made, he couldn't be too dumb. During "Desert Storm" he served with the Marines in Iraq and other Middle Eastern countries. He was mustered out as a Captain. He was apparently in Marine Intelligence. So was McClelland. They both worked from time to time behind the enemy lines. The Marines' records were vague. Blair was awarded a Silver Star, so he must have seen some combat. We were unable to get any details about his service from the Marine's records. As you just said, you know Marine Intelligence. They wouldn't give us the time of day. He may have been operating with one of the other intelligence services, a clandestine organization, to which many Marines and Navy officers were attached.

His business career started with the practice of law in Richmond where he started a law firm with Edmund R. Wainright, III. The firm has a good reputation and presently has about 40 attorneys. It appears prosperous. Although Blair does not appear to be actively practicing law, he still maintains an office at Blair and Wainright.

After a few years of practicing law, he went into business with a number of his clients in the United States and in a number of foreign countries. Most of these businesses have been very successful from a financial viewpoint. He now is a major investor in some fifteen corporations that we know of, including Mercer Metals, a manufacturer of so-called "exotic metals", which are used in many weapons such as nuclear submarines, missiles, rockets, and bombs. He is Chairman and CEO. Because of this we believe he has a Top Secret clearance. I was not able to check this. He has a substantial net worth. We found no debts, except the usual current expenses, and he appears to have been paying these in a timely manner.

"His hobbies: he collects and restores old cars, plays golf- shoots in the nineties. Does some trap and skeet shooting. Apparently he

Escape from Iran

is in good health. Also goes bird hunting. However, his real thrust seems to be working with his various businesses. In addition to his interest in the metals business, he has interests in coal, railroading, publishing (he owns part of magazine published in London, which is aimed at the diplomatic corps), and quite a few other businesses. These businesses have taken him over much of the world. He has or has had interests in businesses located in Mexico, the Dominican Republic, the People's Republic of China, England, Belgium, and other countries. He's probably a pretty savvy person and will be wary of working for us. Details of our investigation, including the names of persons interviewed, are attached. Nothing bad."

Sampson, reading from his copy of the report, "I see from the attached bank statements and tax returns that Blair is indeed very wealthy. I'm not sure he would want to get involved in something like this. We'll have to figure some way to get him to work for us. In my opinion we will have a very difficult time attempting to explain to a person like Blair that we want him to work for the CIA."

Cabot paused and took a sip of coffee, "From my conversations with the President, I'm sure that he would be most willing to help us recruit Blair. Blair will be perfect. The Iranians would not expect a person such as Blair to be working for us. I'll talk to the President when I brief him tomorrow. As you know, the President can be very persuasive. In the meantime, if any of you have any good ideas, please let me know."

For a brief moment Cabot gazed out of the conference room window. The sun was now shining brightly in a cloudless sky. Maybe it was a good omen. Without another word Cabot rose from his seat at the end of the table, picked up his coffee cup and the papers in front of him, and disappeared through the double doors to his private office. The others knew the meeting was over.

CHAPTER 5.

THE MONDAY BEFORE THANKSGIVING

Robert Alexander Blair was 38 years old, a handsome man, six feet one inch tall with a full head of dark brown hair, graying at the temples, but that was not the reason everyone thought he had it made. He was very rich. He had a lovely wife, three beautiful homes, an apartment in New York City, chauffeured automobiles and several airplanes at his disposal, and many of the other trappings of wealth. He owned all or part of a considerable number of businesses both in the United States and abroad, including a large plant in Pennsylvania, which manufactured so called "exotic metals" for the Government's nuclear energy and defense programs.

While he continued to work hard, his life was very busy and satisfying. Still, he looked forward to the annual Thanksgiving holiday, which he would spend with his wife and family at their farm near Ligonier, in western Pennsylvania.

Little did Alex Blair know that several meetings in Washington, D.C., some 150 miles away, would soon change his life.

CHAPTER 5

THE FRIDAY AFTER THANKSGIVING

Alex Blair was enjoying his Thanksgiving holiday. It was a nice change of pace from the busy schedule he maintained. He and his wife, Elizabeth, had arrived at their farm in Ligonier, Pennsylvania, on Wednesday evening. The whole family had gathered on Thursday for the annual ritual of football games on TV and a big Thanksgiving dinner, catered by the local country club.

Friday was cold, bleak and rainy, but it was nice and quiet. His children and guests had departed. There was a nice, warm fire in the fireplace of the cozy living room, and Alex was able to catch up on some of the paperwork he had brought with him in his old, battered briefcase, a gift many years before from his wife's father. He particularly wanted to prepare himself for Monday's meeting on his pending acquisition of the PC&R Railroad.

PC&R was the largest deal in which Alex had ever been involved. PC&R was a major railroad with over two thousand miles of track

Escape from Iran

between several major Midwestern and Canadian industrial areas. It owned some thirty thousand coal and freight cars, which at this time were in demand and heavily utilized at a substantial profit. PC&R also owned hotels, shopping centers, and vast tracts of land under laid by coal and other valuable minerals. It was very profitable. The only reason it was for sale was that its parent company, a major Swiss conglomerate, was in bankruptcy.

Alex worked for an hour or so, and then he decided to get some fresh air and do some bird hunting. It was not too great a day. It was rainy and cool, almost chilly. However, he felt he needed to get out of the house and get some exercise. He also wanted to inspect the hedgerows that he had planted the previous summer. The hedgerows and other ground cover had been planted at considerable expense in hopes of bringing in birds, but the plantings had not been too successful in doing this. The plantings grew all right, but no birds came. It was believed that the foxes ate the birds' eggs and drove the birds away. However, he liked to inspect the farm at every chance he had. He had purchased the eight hundred acres some ten years ago and had added a few improvements every year or so.

Alex and his old Golden Retriever, Jeremiah, had just finished the hunt. *Hiking* would probably be a better word. *Jeremiah was a retriever, not a Pointer.* They had not flushed one bird, but Alex had enjoyed the exercise and getting out in the open. He came out of the woods at the top of the ridge to the west of the farmhouse. The weather had cleared up. The rain had stopped. From there he could see down the valley for miles, all the way to the Laurel Mountains in the distance. Alex noticed the white and blue Pennsylvania state police car coming up the farm road followed by a black station wagon. "I wonder what's up." He momentarily mused. He unloaded his shotgun and started the long walk down the hill to the farmhouse.

When he arrived he noticed that the two cars were parked in front of the house. A Pennsylvania state trooper and two men in dark blue overcoats were lounging in front of the station wagon. He also noticed that the big Chevrolet station wagon had U.S. government license plates.

"Are you, Mr. Blair?" one of the men in overcoats asked.

"Yes. What's going on?" Alex answered.

"Secretary Elbridge from Washington is in here to see you. He'll explain everything. He's inside."

The name Elbridge sounded familiar to Alex, but he could not place it. and he wondered why would a Secretary from Washington be coming to see him?

He entered the farmhouse, carefully leaned his shotgun in the corner next to an old World War I shell casing containing several walking sticks, a cane and a number of umbrellas. He took off his

Escape from Iran

Barbour jacket and hung it on a peg in a closet by the front door. He then followed the aroma of coffee and burning logs into the living room. A rather imposing man, impeccably dressed in a dark suit and white shirt, was standing with his back to the fire.

"Alex, this is Secretary Elbridge", said Elizabeth, his wife. "He's come to…"

"Mr. Blair. Carlton Elbridge", the visitor interrupted, holding out his hand. "The President has sent me to talk with you. I'd like to have a few moments with you. Alone, if Mrs. Blair will excuse us."

"Certainly," said Elizabeth, her tone showing she was somewhat annoyed at being so summarily dismissed. "If you will excuse me, there's fresh coffee on the table. I'll be in the kitchen, if you need anything."

Elizabeth left the room.

"Please sit down", said Elbridge.

Alex sat down. He was very puzzled and somewhat annoyed to be told to sit down in his own home.

"I'm the Assistant Secretary of State for Middle Eastern Affairs. The President has sent me to talk with you. What I will discuss with you must remain confidential. In fact, it is top-secret. You must not discuss it with anyone, including your wife or family. Do you agree to do this?"

"Yes," answered a very perplexed Alex.

"This concerns Iran and a person we'll not name for now."

G. Gray Garland

Alex still did not understand. "I've never been to Iran. I do not know anyone there," replied Alex rather weakly.

"We know that! We know you have never been there," snapped Eldridge still standing, "but that's not important. Please listen to what I have to say." Let me continue. This matter is so secret that any word of it would jeopardize many lives. Before I continue I must have your word that what I tell you will remain secret, top-secret, between us. Do you agree?"

"Yes, sure, I agree. What the hell is this all about?"

"Very well," said Elbridge, who was now sitting in Alex's favorite chair. Elbridge reaching into a small black leather briefcase at his feet, continued, "I must ask you to sign this paper, confirming your promise to maintain the secrecy of what I say." With that he handed the paper to Alex.

Alex was annoyed at this request, but he felt he should at least find out what all this was about.

"You're a lawyer, so you'll understand what you are signing. If I offend you by asking this, I can only apologize. National Security regulations require it."

Alex looked up from reading the paper and placed it on the coffee table in front of him. "What if I refuse to sign this?"

28

Escape from Iran

The Secretary smiled for the first time. "I'll proceed anyway, and hope that you will keep your word. We've checked you very carefully. I know you're a man of your word and a true patriot."

Eldridge stood up again and started to pace. He seemed just a little too edgy to Alex. Perhaps he was concerned about Alex's reaction. "Mr. Blair, this will involve your going to Iran for us to perform a job for the Government. There will, of course, be some danger, but we feel we can minimize it."

"I can't go to Iran. You should know that! We were lucky to get the hostages out of there. Americans are unwelcome. It would be suicide for me or anyone like me to set foot there."

Elbridge raised his voice." Hold on! Hold on! Wait until I explain things to you! All I want you say now is that you'll consider it. If you agree to that, I want you to go back to Washington with me. We'll go over this fully, and then you can say 'Yes' or 'No'. This mission has the highest priority, and we'll leave no stone unturned to make it successful. In fact, it is so important that the President himself wants to talk with you."

Alex's mind was racing ahead *"Why do they need a 38 year-old businessman -lawyer, for a secret mission into an extremely hostile country. God, the way they run the government! I could easily be a sacrificial lamb.*

Once I get in there, how can I get out? It took years to get the hostages out, and Lord knows how many Americans are still there after all these years, still being held captive."

The Secretary droned on. Alex was concentrating so hard on his own thoughts that he barely heard what was being said.

"...and if this is satisfactory, I would like for you fly down the Washington with me now. I have a plane at Latrobe airport. We could be there in about an hour. Meet the President, listen to the project, and make up your mind. If you agree to go ahead, you'll be doing your country a great service. If you decide you don't want to do it, there will be no hard feelings. In any event, we can fly you back here tonight."

Every instinct told Alex to say "No", but he heard himself saying, "Yes, I'll come to Washington and listen."

As they left the farm, a drizzle turned into a light snow. With the State Police car in the lead, the two cars followed State Route 711 to Ligonier and proceeded west on US 30 to Latrobe Airport. Elbridge appeared tired and made no attempt at conversation, except to say he had been to Ligonier several times to play golf at Laurel Valley Golf Club and how pretty he thought the area was.

The cars turned into the airport, went through a gate next to the terminal and followed a taxiway to a remote area of the field. Awaiting them was a large blue and white jet with gold trim, the colors of the White House fleet. Alex had a lump in his throat. *"A Gulfstream IV,"*

Escape from Iran

he thought. Three or four snappy looking airmen in their blue uniform coats were guarding the plane. Alex noticed that several of them carried sidearms and one had an M16 slung over his shoulder. This seemed odd in an area where many people never even locked their doors. The airmen saluted as the Secretary boarded the plane followed by Alex. The engines were already revving up as they reached the seats that Eldbridge with a wave of his arm, indicated they should occupy.

Alex looked around. The plane's furnishings were quite luxurious. There were several couches with coffee tables and end tables with lamps on them. It was like a well-furnished living room. There were even two telephones, one red and one blue, and a large screen TV. Alex had been on some really nice private planes, but this one was really plush.

Two young men in dark suits with white shirts and regimental ties appeared as if on cue. The Secretary did not bother to introduce them.

"Tell Communications we'll arrive at Andrews in about 30 minutes. We should be at the White House in about another 30 minutes depending on traffic. It's a holiday and traffic should be light."

"Yes, Sir."

The thought suddenly came to Alex. *"You know, I never did sign the confidentiality paper. If it was all that important, I'd like to know why Elbridge forgot to ask me to sign it."*

CHAPTER 6

The White House was very impressive. Alex was in awe of the Oval Office, and meeting the President was something else. He could not understand why he felt very nervous talking with the President. He had talked with other famous people without having the butterflies he now had.

The President was friendly. He even called Alex by his first name.

There was a minute or two of small talk. "It is nice of you to take time from your holiday to come and see me, Alex. We need your help with this Iranian mess. I know I can depend on you to help your President and your country."

Before Alex could really say "Yes" or "No" or ask, "Help with what?" The President said, "Thanks! I knew we could depend on you. Goodbye and good luck. Secretary Elbridge will explain everything." And with that Alex was whisked out of the Oval Office and down a hallway to a well-furnished but somewhat smaller office.

Escape from Iran

Two men were waiting in the office. One wore a sweater. The other had on a somewhat rumpled tweed jacket with no tie, a dress shirt open at the collar and scruffy loafers. They both appeared as if they had been summoned from their own holidays without much warning.

Elbridge introduced them. "This is Jeffrey Sherman of the National Security Council and Robert Gordon of the Central Intelligence Agency. They will brief you on the project and where you fit into it. Since I am familiar with it already, I am going to have to leave you for a few moments. I have to take care of some pressing matters. I'll be back as soon as I can."

With that Assistant Secretary Eldbridge left. Alex never saw him again.

Robert Gordon, an athletic looking man in his mid forties. The one in the tweed jacket, was a six-foot athletic looking person. Gordon spoke. "The code name for this project is "Fish Hook". The primary mission of the project is to locate the Ayatollah Montazeri and to transport him from Iran to the United States."

"And you want my help?" stammered a very puzzled Alex rather weakly.

Robert Gordon continued, "First, let me ask you something. You know Robert McClelland! You went to Virginia Military Institute with him. You were in the Marines with him. We believe that you were good friends. Is this true?"

33

Alex suddenly remembered a call he had received just last week at his office in New York. The caller had said he was from the Alumni Office at VMI. He was trying to update records and wanted to know about McClelland. So that's how they had verified this.

"Yes, that's true, but I haven't seen him in many years. Maybe ten or twenty. I don't even know where he is."

"We do! He is in Iran. He is an advisor to the Ayatollah Marzai."

"He's what?" Alex swallowed hard. "*I can't believe this. This has to be a bad dream.*"

"Let me continue," said Robert Gordon.

"How do I fit into the picture?" interrupted Alex.

"We want you to renew your friendship with your friend McClelland, and arrange to be invited by him to Iran."

"Why don't you contact him yourself? You don't need me."

"We have tried to contact McClelland, but every attempt has been very unsuccessful. He is suspicious of anyone that he does not know. That's why we have come to you. As best we can tell, he has not returned to the States in over ten to twelve years."

Robert Gordon continued, "We do know that he buys armaments and other supplies for Iran. He appears to live very well. He has a large home in Tehran, and he appears to be free to come and go as he pleases."

Escape from Iran

"I thought that you fellows knew everything or could find everything out." countered Alex.

"You'd be surprised at how much we don't know. Part of our secret is to make people think we know more than we actually do." Robert Gordon chuckled and continued, "McClelland likes women, but we've not been able to entice him with any of our agents, and, believe me, some of them could make you leave home."

Alex spoke, "Why don't you have someone from our Embassy contact him?"

"Well, our Embassy in Tehran is closed, as you know."

"No, I mean when he goes to some place outside of Iran."

"We've thought of that, but we are somewhat afraid if we do contact him that way, it may destroy his potential usefulness to us."

"But, why me? Don't you have other people who know him as well I do? "

"No, you would be surprised. There are only two or three of you that we have come up with. Two of his friends are dead, and the other living one is a well-known politician. We feel he is too high profile for us to involve him."

"You mean Senator Harrison?"

"Yes, that's who we mean."

"How do you expect me to succeed? Is this possible? If I contacted him now after all these years, he'd know I had an ulterior motive."

35

G. Gray Garland

"We don't think that would be a problem," Robert Gordon continued.

"McClelland does not often leave Iran, but he usually makes three or four trips a year to Paris. He always stays at the same hotel, The Athenee Palace. He is usually busy doing his business during the day. He visits with banks, arms dealers, exporters and others. Some of what he does we know about. Some we do not. He is very careful and apparently will not even talk or deal with anyone he does not know. At night he likes to go out to dinner, usually at one of the better restaurants. What we want is to arrange for you to meet him by chance and renew your friendship. We can find out when he is coming to Paris, because the Athenee Palace is usually so booked up that he has to make reservations in advance."

"We want you to be in Paris when he next comes there," continued Robert Gordon. "We want you to bump into him as if it were a coincidence. Nature can then run its course."

"When will he be in Paris again?" asked Alex.

"We really don't know, but we think any day now. He hasn't been there since last spring. We must be ready to move at a moment's notice."

"All you want me to do is renew my friendship? You must want me to do more than just that."

Escape from Iran

Gordon paused for a moment and then he continued, "What we really want to know is whether there is any chance of our turning McClelland, so that he will work for us."

"Then basically all I have to do is find out whether or not Bob would be willing to work for the United States. If I meet him in Paris, maybe I can find that out without having to go to Iran."

"That could be true. Let's just see how things go."

With that the meeting ended, and Gordon arranged to have Alex driven back to Andrews Field for his flight back to Ligonier.

CHAPTER 7

THE SATURDAY AFTER THANKSGIVING

It was the next day, Saturday. Alex was back at his farm. Jeremiah lay in front of the fireplace absorbing the heat from the burning logs. Usually Jeremiah would be sleeping by the fire , but today he watched Alex expectantly, sensing his master's restive mood.

Yesterday Alex had been enjoying a relaxed Thanksgiving Holiday, that is until Secretary Elbridge arrived and whisked him off to Washington.

Today he was still getting over the events of yesterday, the visit of Elbridge, meeting the President and being asked to go to Paris to meet McClelland.

Alex placed the heavy black briefing book they had given him with its "Top Secret" markings on the coffee table, stood up, stretched, and put another log on the fire. He went to the window and looked outside. It was raining hard, but he was so deep in thought that he hardly noticed. Many thoughts raced through his mind.

Escape from Iran

Alex wondered why the President never mentioned the mission. *Was he trying to keep his distance from it, in the event it fails, and I am caught by the Iranians? If he was questioned about what the President said, he could not truly say that the President said anything about the mission or asked him to do anything. Is McClelland a spy for the CIA or is he a traitor?" This was a question he had failed to ask in the excitement of the meetings in Washington.*

Robert Gordon had said that once Alex renewed his friendship with McClelland, he should try to persuade McClelland to return to the United States and bring with him one more of the top Iranian scientists. Alex should tell McClelland that he thought he might be able to work something out, so that McClelland would not face criminal charges for being a traitor.

Alex wondered, *"How can McClelland help to get anyone out of Iran, even if he is willing to help, which in my opinion is doubtful?"*

He looked down at the heavy black book on McClelland. It brought back many memories of the old days at VMI and in the Marines with McClelland and many others.

Alex had a good feeling about Robert Gordon. He instinctively liked him. He recalled that Gordon seemed open and honest in discussing the project. He did not seem to avoid answering any of the questions that Alex had asked. Yet Alex had butterflies in his stomach when he thought about the project. *Would he be jeopardizing an old friend? Would I be in danger of losing my life? I really don't need this*

39

aggravation. How can I say no to the President of the United States? What can I do? Maybe I can go to Paris and say I'm not going to Iran. Maybe I will not be invited. That would be good,

CHAPTER 8

SUNDAY AFTER THANKSGIVING

Eight time zones to the East, Robert McClelland strolled out of the double doors from his library onto the large veranda of his luxurious home overlooking Tehran. It was a beautiful night, cool, crisp and clear.

McClelland was depressed. Holidays, especially American holidays, depressed him. He had just seen a film clip on the CNN nightly news about the Thanksgiving holidays in the United States. Times like these left him feeling lonely and isolated. But, of course, there were compensations. Since coming to Iran he had amassed a fortune of almost $900 million, and he had a magnificent home in Iran, servants, cars, planes, paintings and all the things money could buy. But he did not have any close friends. McClelland never felt as if he belonged. Any wrong move on his part, and he would probably be tortured to death. It wasn't the life he had envisioned.

G. Gray Garland

His Iranian associates were nice enough to him, but he would never really be a part of their society. He felt he was more or less tolerated because of his ability to procure armaments and other hard-to-obtain goods. They did not seem to mind the fact that he was an American. However, their attitude would likely change dramatically if he moved somewhere else to live, particularly to America or a country friendly to America.

McClelland remembered past Thanksgiving holidays. He could not figure out why they depressed him. Even as a child growing up in Tennessee they meant little or nothing. Maybe that was why.

From an early age his father had raised him. He had no memory of his mother. His father never discussed her, and on the few occasions when McClelland asked about her, his father never really answered. his questions. His father was good to him, and McClelland loved him dearly. The elder McClelland, while attentive to the basic needs of his son, was not very communicative. He always seemed to be deep in his thoughts, brooding about the past and worrying about the future. He had no job, but always appeared to have an adequate income to meet their modest needs. They usually ate at home, but sometimes they might celebrate Thanksgiving or other holidays by going to a nearby restaurant for dinner. However, holidays were never a big deal.

It was during his freshman or "rat" year at VMI when he was suddenly called home by a neighbor, who told McClelland that his

Escape from Iran

father had been shot by a burglar and was in the local hospital. He had been shot as he sat reading in his den. The neighbor told McClelland the police had told him McClelland's father probably would have been killed, if a Nashville police car had not been passing the house just as the first shot was fired. The two policemen from the patrol car chased the shooter, but he got away in the darkness.

When McClelland went to the hospital, the doctor told him that his father would survive. He had been shot in the shoulder. By a miracle the bullet had not damaged any vital parts.

At the hospital McClelland noticed that his father's room was guarded by two uniformed policemen. It was then that he learned the truth.

As he was coming out of his father's hospital room, he was approached by a well dressed, clean-cut man of about forty-five. "Mr. McClelland, may I speak with you." McClelland nodded affirmatively. *He must be from the police.*

"I'm Sam Pringle. I would like to talk to you about your father." He produced a card and badge, but McClelland was too distracted to examine it. "Let's go to the cafeteria and have a cup of coffee."

They walked in silence to the elevator and did not resume talking until they were seated with their coffee in a corner of the nearly deserted hospital cafeteria. "I'm glad your father will be all right. We've been friends for a long time. I guess the only way to approach what I have to tell you is to dive in and be blunt. I'm with the Central Intelligence Agency. I have identification, if you care to see it. You didn't seem interested when I showed it to you upstairs."

McClelland said nothing. Sam continued, "Your father worked for us many years ago. He did some things that annoyed people in high places. I need not go into that now, but these people wanted your father eliminated. They made one attempt, but missed your father and killed your mother."

McClelland was too shocked to do anything but listen.

"Sometime later your father retired on a pension, and he relocated here. However, the people after him have long memories. Somehow they found out he was living here. They sent a hit man here to kill your father. Fortunately we found out. Don't ask me how, and we made arrangements to guard your father. Unfortunately the assassin slipped by our guards and got to the window of your house. Just as he was about to fire through the window, one of our guards spotted him. The guard realized he could not draw his pistol fast enough to shoot the assassin before he shot your father, but he really used his head. He yelled in a loud voice, 'Stop! Police!' This apparently distracted the assassin so that he missed your father with his first shot. But being a cool professional he aimed and fired a second shot. Your father hearing the first shot had jumped up, and this shot hit him in the shoulder rather than in the head.

Escape from Iran

The assassin did not get to fire a third shot at your father. By then the first guard had pumped two shots at him and a second guard was running up the driveway. The assassin had to cut and run. Both guards fired at him, but it was dark. and he was apparently not hit. Within minutes the area was cordoned off by the Nashville police, but the assassin had escaped."

Two months later the assassin did not miss, and McClelland was alone.

CHAPTER 9

MONDAY, NOVEMBER 28, 1983

The Monday after Thanksgiving Alex flew to New York to work on the PC&R merger. Some months previously, in April to be exact, Alex had been approached by an associate in his Richmond office to help a group attempting to acquire the Pittsburgh, Conemaugh and Rochester Railroad Corporation, sometimes called the PC&R.

PC&R was a Pittsburgh, Pennsylvania, based conglomerate, which owned and operated one of the United States' major railroads. It also was involved in manufacturing, repairing and leasing railcars, and it was a major owner of land and commercial real estate, including shopping malls and hotels. Additionally, it had a history of being very profitable. It was for sale because its parent corporation was in financial trouble.

A group of Pittsburgh investors had been trying to obtain financing to purchase the conglomerate without success for some time and felt that Alex with his connections could help them. They had offered Alex a substantial interest, if he would join them and help with the

Escape from Iran

financing. Alex had contacted a number of banks and insurance companies without success, but Walter Bortz, a Swiss banker, he had met at a party in New York had helped to arrange the financing, not through a Swiss Bank, as Alex had anticipated, but through New York National Bank.

CHAPTER 10

THE FIRST FRIDAY IN DECEMBER

The following weekend, by prearrangement, Alex went to Virginia for further briefings. Robert Gordon arranged to have Alex picked up at LaGuardia Airport about noon on Friday. Alex's driver, Walter, picked him up at the apartment on East Fifty-sixth Street and drove him to the terminal for private aircraft. At the terminal he was met by a clean cut young man, obviously a pilot. "Mr. Blair, I'm Joe Gibson. Mr. Gordon sent me to pick you up. Give me your bag, and we will go out to the plane."

Alex noticed that the plane was a Beechcraft King Air with no special markings on it other than the required numbers. They immediately took off and flew directly to a small airfield near Culpeper, Virginia. There an unmarked Ford Crown Victoria sedan with Virginia license plates picked him up and drove him to what appeared to be a prosperous country estate. They drove through the gates and up a long, tree lined driveway to a handsome, white columned brick house.

Escape from Iran

Robert Gordon met him on the front steps. He was neatly dressed in a tweed sport coat with dress slacks and shined loafers. To Alex Gordon he appeared every inch the country squire meeting one of his weekend guests.

"Thank you for coming down, Alex. Come in, and we'll get you settled."

Alex was then shown by Gordon to a nicely furnished suite of rooms on the second floor.

"When you've had a chance to freshen up, come down to the library, and we'll get started."

Pretty posh for a government facility. Do they use this to persuade people like me to do something they really don't want to do.

Alex unpacked and changed to a sport coat and khaki slacks all the while wondering what he was getting into. *Why do they need a mansion like this? Why are they wining and dining me? Leading the pig to slaughter? I had better be very careful. They aren't looking out for my best interests. I like Gordon, but can I really trust him?*

When Alex entered the library he was introduced to a handsome, grey haired man who stood by the fireplace. "This is Howard Berkley ", said Gordon. Howard is with the State Department. He is very knowledgeable about Iran and the conditions you may encounter there. Let's have some lunch. We can talk while we eat."

49

G. Gray Garland

They proceeded into a very luxuriously appointed dining room with floor to ceiling windows looking over the lovely Virginia countryside. They were served a simple luncheon of soup, sandwiches and coffee.

During the luncheon Howard Berkley briefed Alex about conditions in Iran. He talked about many things, including, with much emphasis, the intense hostility towards Americans.

After lunch they returned to the library where a dark skinned, nattily dressed young man about five foot eight inches tall, awaited them. Gordon merely introduced him as Mohammed Azar. Gordon did not say for whom Azar worked or what he did.

The three of them spent much of the afternoon reviewing more information on Iran. They discussed the structure of its government, who is who, the various groups of terrorists, and about certain embassies where Alex might find help in an emergency. Robert Gordon had two massive black notebooks, but most of the information on Iran and what to expect there came from Mohammed.

They took a break about four o'clock for coffee and cakes. After that Robert Gordon said, "We're now going to play a serious game. We shall be the Iranians, and we shall question you about your willingness to sell metals to us."

Both Howard Berkley and Mohammed Azar started to drill Alex with questions they thought the Iranians might ask him when he was there. Questions such as: "How much do you charge for this metal

50

Escape from Iran

specification and for that one?" Alex was amazed at how much they knew about his business and the different metal he made.

Gordon chimed in, "Alex, be sure you tell the truth with respect to your prices. If I know the Iranians, they will already know what you're charging."

Berkley resumed his questions, "Are you aware that there are sanctions against your selling metals to Iran? Would you be willing to sell products to a third party in a country where there are no sanctions against selling your metal, even if you knew or suspected the product would be resold to Iran? What if we made it very profitable for you personally to sell metals to us?"

Alex interrupted, "I am not going to get involved with that, unless I have something from you in writing, giving me immunity, and this writing will have to be executed by the Attorney General or perhaps the President."

Berkley stopped to sip his drink, wipe his mouth on the back of his hand and then continued, "If your selling some metals to the Iranians becomes necessary to your mission, we can arrange for you to have that."

"We can arrange that, if it becomes necessary," replied Gordon.

After that the questions came rapidly and answers together with discussions and comments on how to answer them went on for several hours.

51

G. Gray Garland

Alex was very impressed. It seemed to Alex that every contingency must have been discussed. He could not think of any question the Iranians might ask him for which he had not been given an answer. They then terminated the meeting and agreed to meet for dinner in about an hour.

Alex had listened carefully and tried to absorb everything that had been said. But he thought to himself, *When you sum it all up, what they're saying simply means that Iran is one hell of a dangerous place, especially for an American and even more so for an intelligence agent. Why are they briefing me with all of this Iranian information, when I may be able to accomplish what they want by merely meeting McClellan in Paris. I may not have to go to Iran. It does not make a lot of sense to me."*

During the break before dinner, Alex called his answering machines both at his New York and Richmond offices. It was too late to expect that anyone was still working. He wanted to check on his calls and any business transactions, particularly news about the pending acquisition of PC&R. Both offices had left messages that there was nothing new, so Alex did not feel guilty that he was not at the office. In any event it was Friday, and Alex did not believe anything would happen over the weekend.

The next morning when Alex returned to the library after eating breakfast alone, Robert Gordon was there. As Alex entered, he said, "Get your coat, Alex. We are going to take a ride."

Escape from Iran

A few minutes later they took off from the front of the house in a grey Jeep Grand Cherokee station wagon with Gordon driving. They arrived at a large stone barn. However, once inside Alex saw it was obviously not a barn, but some sort of combination of offices, laboratories and a factory. They went into a Spartan conference room furnished with grey metal furniture.

Within a minute or two a tall thin man in his mid-to-late fifties wearing a lab smock entered the room. Robert Gordon introduced him. "This is John Gilman, who will be working on the technical side of our project. We cannot send a radio in with you because we are afraid that it would be discovered, and it would blow your cover. However, we hope to be able to get a radio into your hands. We'll give you the name of a shop or restaurant. You'll go there, as a normal tourist, and the radio will be slipped to you as part of your purchase. So now we shall show you how to operate it. We feel that you should be familiar with its operations."

The next twenty-five minutes were spent familiarizing Alex with several models of radios used by the CIA. John Gilman explained their operation, their ranges, etc. Alex was most impressed by a radio imbedded in an ordinary wristwatch.

As he concluded Gilman said, "Before you undertake your mission, you will be briefed on codes, best times of transmissions. That is not our job here. I'll leave you now. Good luck."

Another middle-aged man joined them. He too was wearing a white smock and looked every inch the scientist that he probably was. He was introduced as Mr. Hanratty. He put a black briefcase on the table and proceeded to open it. Alex watched in puzzlement. The briefcase appeared empty. Mr. Hanratty began to dissemble parts of the briefcase and placed an object on the table.

Hanratty explained, "This is a cellular telephone which works off of a satellite. It works like the wrist watch you were just shown."

Alex was puzzled,"Other than being able to hide it, what's so unusual about this?"

Then Mr. Hanratty showed Alex. "It's a satellite radio. If you dial your code, which let's say is '1,2,3', and then talk into the phone, it will record what you have said. Then at a later time when you make a regular phone call, if you press this button while talking, the phone will silently transmit your secret message to the person receiving the call. In other words, you can call up and say to your wife, 'How are the children, etc.' By pressing the preset code button, the phone will make an almost imperceptible noise which sounds like a quick burst of static. The receiver will record the static and place the cassette in one of these machines. The burst is stretched out so that the receiver can hear your secret message. Very clever, isn't it?"

"It sure is, but how do you find the satellite?" replied an amazed Alex.

Escape from Iran

"You will know the general location of the satellite, so you aim the invisible antenna in that direction and move it about until this green light lights comes on and stops blinking . You more or less tune it like an FM radio. The satellite gives out a homing signal when it is expecting a call, so you tune in on it."

"Couldn't the Russians tune in and intercept our messages?"

"Yes, they probably can. However, each radio has a computer chip that scrambles the quick burst transmission. Without a similar chip it is virtually impossible to decipher the message."

Alex was impressed, but Hanratty wasn't finished. He picked up another item from the table in front of him.

"Here is a small penlight, the size of a pen. Here, try it."

Alex pressed the button and the bulb lit up. He was puzzled. It was just an ordinary pen light. In fact, it even had an advertising logo on its case advertising a sand and gravel company in Virginia.

"Now," he said, taking the flashlight from Alex, "Watch this. We reverse the batteries and I press the button."

He aimed the flashlight in the direction of a sandbox with a thick piece of wood lying on the sand. He pressed the button and there was a loud report and the piece of wood now had a large hole in it.

"When the batteries are inserted in the proper order, this functions as a flashlight. When you reverse the batteries, it functions as a single-shot pistol. Each battery is also a cartridge that will fire when it is reversed and you press on the switch. So be very careful that the batteries are put in the way you want them."

Alex, who liked gadgets, enjoyed his time at the laboratory.

When they returned to the house it was almost seven o'clock. Robert Gordon suggested a drink. Alex readily accepted. It had been a very full day.

"Dewars and soda with a twist of lemon for you?"

"Yes, that'll be great". *How does he know what I drink? God, I wonder how much else he knows?*

"Alex, we've been thinking about your missions, and we feel that when you go to Paris you should take a secretary with you. She will be one of our people, of course. We know McClelland likes women, perhaps a good looking secretary will enhance your ability to accomplish the mission."

The double doors to the library opened as if on some cue, and a young woman entered the room. Alex was absolutely stunned. One of the most beautiful women he had ever seen was entering the room.

Robert Gordon with a sly smile on his face said, "Alex, I want you to meet Patricia Diaz."

CHAPTER 11

Patricia Diaz was a truly beautiful, stunning blue-eyed, blonde about five feet, eight inches tall with the figure of a movie star. She had been born in Spain twenty-six years ago. She was the eldest of two daughters of three children-two girls and a boy. Her brother was born much later, and her father treated her as a son. The father was from a wealthy Spanish family and her mother was from an even wealthier American family of Irish descent. With her lovely complexion and striking figure, she could easily have been a fashion model or a movie star. Her father, who was only twenty-three when she was born, had been a famous bullfighter and continued to love the outdoors, particularly riding and hunting. He maintained a stable of polo ponies and hunted game all over the world. The family's main home was a very large estancia in Argentina. The family also maintained homes in southern Spain and in the United States.

Patricia, the first born, was in the early days the son her father had never had. At a very young age she had learned to ride and shoot. By the time she was sixteen she had been on many hunting trips with her father and even had her pilot's license.

Her mother had attended Hollins College in Roanoke, Virginia, so at her mother's urging Patricia also went there. In the beginning she admitted the only thing she really liked about the college was that she could take two of her horses to college with her.

Patricia was also very intelligent and easily made good grades at Hollins. Since she had turned into an extraordinarily beautiful girl, she had her share of suitors from nearby colleges, such as The University of Virginia, Washington & Lee, and Virginia Military Institute, but there had been no serious romances. Strangely her beauty and wealth appeared to be a deterrent to the few boys to whom she was attracted.

During her senior year she visited a classmate in Warrenton, Virginia, to ride in a fox hunt. There she met Ronald Cassidy, a senior at the Law School at Washington and Lee, whose parents had a large estate outside of Warrenton. Virginia.

Patricia began dating Ronald Cassidy. Ronald's family was originally from California where his father had made a considerable fortune by investing in a number of very successful high tech companies. The Cassidy family spent most of their weekends and holidays at their Warrenton estate, but during most weekdays they week lived in the Georgetown section of Washington D.C., where Ronald, Sr. was a Deputy Director of the Central Intelligence Agency.

Escape from Iran

The Cassidys had a lovely home in Warrenton, which Patricia frequently visited. Patricia relished the "horsey" atmosphere and riding to the hounds with the Warrenton Hunt. During one of her visits in talking with the elder Cassidy, she recounted how she had solved a crime on the campus at Hollins.

It seemed that there had been a series of thefts from the rooms of the students in her dormitory. This had continued for several months without campus security or the students being able to solve this mystery. Finally Patricia's wristwatch was stolen. It was a birthday gift from her father, and she was very upset at losing it. She reported the theft to the school, but the school said there was little or nothing they could do about it.

She decided to hell with it, she would solve the mystery of the thefts herself. She went to an electronics store in Roanoke where she purchased a mini-television camera and cables. She hid the camera in a light fixture in the hall and ran the cable to her VCR, into which she placed an eight hour tape. She even opened the back of the VCR and disconnected the indicator lights, so that it would not appear to be recording.

The camera was positioned to cover the entire length of the hall, and surely enough, Patricia knew who the thief was when she reviewed the first day's tape. The thief was a student from an adjoining dormitory.

G. Gray Garland

Patricia decided before turning the thief into the authorities she should find out as much about the student as she could. Her inquires revealed that the student came from a very well do to family near Abington, Virginia. Patricia felt there was no valid reason for the student to be stealing.

Accordingly, she went to see the student during the evening of the second day after she had discovered who she was. At first the student, Grace Harrison, denied that she had stolen anything. However when Patricia told her about the television camera and the tape she had recorded, Grace broke down and admitted that she was the thief.

Further questioning of Grace revealed that she still had in her possession all of the items she had stolen. As the conversation continued, it became obvious that Grace was obviously terrified that she would not only be thrown out of school but also that she would go to jail for her crimes. Patricia felt that Grace should be punished, but she did not feel she wanted to ruin the girl's life for a first offense. Accordingly she said, "If you will return all the items which you have stolen, including my watch, and resign from the college, I will forget this ever happened."

Grace and Patricia arranged to have the stolen items placed in a cardboard box and left anonymously in the office of the Bursar.

Grace resigned, and the matter was mostly forgotten until Patricia told Mr. Cassidy about it. He seemed quite impressed with Patricia's energy and ingenuity, and said, "Patricia when you get out of Hollins,

Escape from Iran

if you ever need a job, come and see me. The CIA really needs people like you."

"When you finish college and need a job, come see me" became sort of a personal joke between them until one weekend late in her senior year when Mr. Cassidy inquired, "Patricia, when are you graduating? If you ever need a job when you leave college, come and see me."

She quickly replied, "I will be finishing school in two months, and I think I would really like to come and work for you."

"Are you really serious?"

Yes, I am very serious," she replied.

The end result was that when she graduated from Hollins in June, summa cum laude, she went to work for the CIA. There was no difficulty in hiring her because she was a U.S. citizen because of her mother's citizenship. In the beginning Mr. Cassidy was very solicitous about how Patricia was doing. However, when she and Ron broke up in the fall, he seemed to loose interest in her progress.

Patricia had made it clear to the agency that she did not want a secretarial or desk job. She wanted to be a field agent. She was trained accordingly.

Her first assignment was in Argentina where she had grown up. The United States was concerned that another conflict was brewing between Argentina and Britain over the Falkland Islands. She worked for a Spanish firm owned by a friend of her father, and through her family connections she was able to be invited to many diplomatic functions where she met important Argentineans. It was a pretty passive assignment and virtually all of the information that she gathered was already known to the U.S. Government.

Working with Alex was her second assignment.

CHAPTER 12

MONDAY, EARLY DECEMBER

Alex was at his New York apartment. He was up early. He was excited. Today was to be the big day. Today he and his group would sign the final agreements to purchase the PC&R. It was the biggest deal he had ever done. He would be the major shareholder in an $85 million dollar deal, and he projected he could improve the already significant earnings to $45 million annually. It seemed that the negotiations had gone on forever. There had been one complication after another. One day they were optimistic that they were going to acquire the PC&R, The next day they felt like they had lost the deal. He strolled into the living room in his pajamas and bare feet and looked out of the big picture window, which had a great view of New York to the south and over the East River. The sun was just coming up, and it looked like it was going to be a beautiful day. To Alex it seemed to be a good omen.

He then went into the kitchen and prepared himself his usual breakfast, consisting of cold cereal, milk, and orange juice. He then

G. Gray Garland

showered and shaved. He then returned to the bedroom, carefully selecting his clothes, picking a conservative, gray flannel suit, white shirt, and striped Club tie. Alex felt strongly that in business you must dress to fit the occasion..

When he walked out of the front door of the New York apartment building on East 56th Street,, his driver, Walter, and the car were waiting for him. As the limousine left the driveway Alex said, "We're to pick up two people at the Regency Hotel." They stopped at the Park Avenue entrance of the Regency. Walter had to double park. As usual at this time of day, a number of limousines were blocking the curb. This was the time of day for the so-called "Power Breakfast" when the business and political elite of New York met to have breakfast and to be seen. In fact, the president of one of Alex's companies usually had breakfast at the Regency and then rode majestically in the limousine the two or three blocks to their offices at 410 Park Avenue. This amused Alex and Walter no end. Alex usually walked to work from the apartment.

Alex went into the lobby where he spotted David Krantz, a tall grey haired man impeccably dressed. He was the Washington lawyer for PC&R. "Good Morning, Dave. Is Bruce with you?"

"He's checking out. We should be ready to go in a minute."

Escape from Iran

Bruce, a stocky balding man of about forty years of age joined them. He was the negotiator for a Wisconsin company, a partner in the buying group.

Soon the big Cadillac with its three passengers moved swiftly down Park Avenue to 57th Street and across to the west side and down to the Lincoln Tunnel and on to the New Jersey Turnpike. Until they were about half way to Philadelphia they made mostly small talk.

Then Krantz asked, "Alex, how many are there in your group?"

"Let's see. There are four of us plus the Minnetonka Corporation. That's no problem, is it?"

"I don't think so. I want to be careful that we are not considered to be making a public offering without the proper registration."

The car phone buzzed. Walter answered it on the front seat extension. "It's for you, Mr. Blair."

Alex picked up the rear seat extension. It was Robert Gordon. He did not say who he was, but Alex recognized Gordon's voice immediately.

He merely said, "Alex, give me a call as soon as you can. We can't talk on this phone." He then hung up.

"Walter, pull into the next service plaza. I have to make a phone call."

Within minutes they pulled into a plaza. Alex excused himself and went to a telephone booth in the parking area. He dialed the

65

G. Gray Garland

number Robert Gordon had given him earlier. Robert came on the line immediately.

"Alex, we may have a bit of a problem. We just got a report from Paris. McClelland is there now. In fact, he's been there for several days. Don't ask me how we missed it, but we've got to get you over there right away. Gordon continued," You are booked on the Concorde tonight, and you have reservations at the Meurice. Your airline tickets will be at the ticket counter at JFK. We could not get you in The Plaza Athenee .We were afraid that if we pushed too hard, someone might get suspicious. We've also got reservations for Patricia. She's coming up on the shuttle from Washington. I am sorry that we cannot give you more time, but this is the best we can do under the circumstances. When you get there, I would suggest that you spend as much time in the Athenee as you can. Perhaps you have some business contacts or friends that you can ask to come by for lunch or dinner and meet with you, etc., and we can only hope that you bump into McClelland."

"Robert, I am not sure I can leave tonight. I am on my way to a very important meeting in Philadelphia. I'm hoping to sign the papers to buy the Pittsburgh Conemaugh and Rochester Railroad Corporation. I'll try to make it, but I can't guarantee it."

"Alex, this is important. Don't let us down."

Escape from Iran

"Robert, you know I'll do my best." Alex hung up without saying goodbye. His stomach was in knots. This was all he needed now. He could do without this kind of pressure. He had to have a clear head to concentrate on the PC&R deal. He didn't exactly trust David Krantz. For some reason he always seemed to be putting up roadblocks to sabotage the deal. Maybe he thought he was protecting his client. Maybe not.

CHAPTER 13

MONDAY, EARLY DECEMBER

The meeting in Philadelphia was at the Union League Club. Alex, David Krantz, and Bruce Dillon arrived early. They were directed to a sitting room to await the others. Within a few minutes Clark Rice, one of the purchasing group arrived from Pittsburgh. Kenneth Shuttle, president of the holding company that was selling PC&R, followed him shortly. The price had been agreed upon earlier. The Pittsburgh group had outbid a group from Connecticut, so they spent most of the morning ironing out various details.

Alex was nervous. It was difficult keeping his mind on the deal at hand. He hated arguing over petty details. The deal had been made. He kept thinking of how he was going to complete the negotiations now underway and still make the Concorde to Paris on time. By lunchtime a final deal had been hammered out. The parties shook hands. Alex and Clark declined Ken Shuttle's invitation to stay for lunch and left the Club.

Escape from Iran

"Let me take you to the airport. I have a car." Alex said to Clark.

"Are you sure it's not out of the way?"

"No, I'm going to have to fly to New York."

Walter was waiting with the car.

"Walter, we're going to the Philadelphia airport. I have to fly back to New York."

"Excuse me, Clark. I have to make a call." Alex picked up the phone on the divider and dialed his New York apartment. There was no answer.

"Walter, call Mrs. Blair and keep calling until you get her. Tell her to pack a suitcase for me with clothes for a quick trip to Paris. Tell her to take it to Air France at Kennedy Airport. I'm going over on the Concorde. I don't have time to go to the apartment and pack. She'll probably have to take a cab. You will likely not be back in time."

When they reached the Philadelphia airport Alex and Clark parted. Clark was returning to Pittsburgh. Alex had to get a flight to John F. Kennedy Airport. There were no flights to JFK, that would arrive in time, so Alex took a USAir flight to LaGuardia, which was already boarding when he arrived at the gate. The flight was quick and uneventful.

As soon as he was in the terminal he called his apartment. No answer.

69

He tried to call his car, but, as he anticipated, he heard the recorded message, "The vehicle you are calling is either out of range or out of service." Walter was still too far out of New York to receive his call.

Alex then took a cab to JFK. *I sure hope Elizabeth got my message.* He hated the pressure of uncertainties like this. *Oh my Lord! I forgot to tell her to include my passport.* Alex was really becoming anxious.

Traffic was heavy, but it moved rapidly, and Alex was soon at the Air France terminal at Kennedy. Elizabeth was not there, but Patricia Diaz was.

Oh, what will Elizabeth think when she sees Patricia? Why can't things go smoothly without so damned many complications?

Alex explained that he was waiting for his wife to bring his suitcase.

Patricia said, "Since we don't have much time, I'll check us both in while you wait here."

Alex thought, *"She's very diplomatic. All I need is to have Elizabeth upset."*

Within a few minutes Elizabeth arrived looking somewhat harassed. She had his suitcase. Before he could ask, she reached into her purse and said, "Here is your passport. I knew you would need it."

"Alex, I have some bad news. David Krantz called and said to tell you he doesn't think the PC&R deal can go through as proposed. Something about too many shareholders will make it a public offering,

Escape from Iran

and they do not want to register with the SEC. He said to have you call him as soon as you could."

"Last call for Air France Concorde flight to Paris", boomed a loud speaker.

"Alex, be careful. Have a good trip. I love you," Elizabeth said in a tone that meant she obviously was very unhappy at Alex's leaving her.

"I love you too. I'll call you as soon as I get there."

Alex raced for the gate.

CHAPTER 14

TUESDAY EARLY DECEMBER

The flight to Paris was uneventful. Alex felt that he could only make small talk with Patricia. He was afraid to talk about their mission for fear that someone would overhear them, so they talked "small talk."

"How come you choose Hollins College in Roanoke, Virginia?

Patricia laughed, a musical laugh with twinkling blue eyes.

Alex was perplexed. "What's so funny?" Their eyes met momentarily.

" 'How come' is so typical of Virginians," replied Patricia, still chuckling. She continued, "I went to Hollins primarily because my mother and grandmother had gone there. Also it was one of the few colleges where I could take my horses."

They were interrupted by a stewardess serving drinks. Alex took a Dewars scotch and soda, Patricia a glass of white wine.

"But you are not from Virginia," continued Alex, sipping his scotch.

Escape from Iran

"No, but my mother and my grandfather and grandmother were from Virginia. They had a farm near Middleburg, where I spent almost every summer. And as you know, summer in Virginia is winter in Argentina where I grew up, so I feel like I am practically a Virginian myself."

"I am confused," said Alex taking a large gulp of his scotch. "I thought you were an Argentinean, the daughter of a famous bull fighter."

"Yes. That's true. Yes my father was a famous toreador. He was actually Spanish, not Argentinean. He was part of the Spanish royal family, a first cousin of the King, but he loved the excitement of a very active life, He loved fast cars, airplanes, hunting, riding, and polo, all of which fortunately he could afford. He took up bull fighting for fun, and when he excelled at it and became an international hero, at least among the bull fighting nations.

"He didn't like the pomp and ceremony of the royal family, and he didn't like all the publicity that came from his bull fighting. His family owned an estancia in Argentina, and he decided to move there. He had met my mother several years before at a party following a horse show in Warrenton, Virginia. He was no longer bull fighting, and they decided they wanted to move to Argentina to live on the ranch that he owned there.

"As I grew up, we traveled a lot. We went to Spain where my father had family and to Virginia where my mother's parents were living. At an early age I learned at to ride and shoot. Truly, it was a wonderful way to grow up.

"When I reach college age I was sent to Hollins. So, that's my life story. Before going to Hollins I spent a year at the University of Mexico. Otherwise my life was exciting to me, but probably dull to others."

"Tell me about your life, Alex."

Alex hated publicity. He hated to talk about his life and his successes. After listening to Patricia talk about her early life, he felt he had to say something.

"I grew up in Richmond, Virginia, and…" he was interrupted by the booming announcement, "Fasten your seatbelts. We'll be landing at Charles de Gaulle airport in five minutes."

Saved by the bell, thought Alex.

By the time they reached central Paris and checked into the Meurice Hotel, Alex decided it was too late for the cocktail hour, so they elected to go to the Plaza Athenee for dinner. Alex had been there many times before and knew the maitre d', so he had no difficulty in obtaining dinner reservations.

Patricia looked absolutely stunning in her dress. Alex felt very self-conscious. He felt that all of the men in the dining room were

Escape from Iran

staring at them, which was probably true. Somehow it made him very uncomfortable. *What if some friend of Elizabeth's saw him. What would they think? What would they say to Elizabeth?* However, the dinner was very pleasant. The food was excellent. Patricia was an excellent conversationalist, and he enjoyed very much talking with her. She seemed to have an incredible knowledge about almost everything they talked about. Even though they were somewhat tired, they decided to prolong their exposure at the Plaza Athenee and have a nightcap in the bar. As they walked across the lobby, Alex looked up and his heart skipped a beat.

There stood McClelland as big as day, staring at Patricia. McClelland had aged, but Alex had no doubt. It was his old friend. Alex quickly moved forward. McClelland frowned. Two rather large men suddenly stepped between them, and Alex thought, *I'm going to have a problem,* when McClelland suddenly beamed and said "My Lord, Alex Blair. What in the world are you doing here?" The two bodyguards backed off. Alex and Bob embraced.

"I'm here for a day or two on business. How about you?"

McClelland, appearing absolutely delighted to see Alex, replied, "So am I."

Alex said, "Let's go into the bar and have a drink. We can talk there. Oh, I meant to introduce you. This is Patricia Diaz, who works with me."

75

G. Gray Garland

McClelland smiled. "I'm very pleased to meet you. Any friend of Alex's is a friend of mine."

The three of them started off in the direction of the bar. Alex noticed that three or four men in dark suits followed along at a discreet distance. When they were seated the men split up with two sitting at a table to his left and two sitting several tables to his right. They were obviously McClelland's bodyguards.

The two old friends began."Alex, where do you live now?"

"I live in Richmond, Virginia,, but I spend a lot of time in New York where I have an office. How about you?"

"I live in Iran."

Alex tried to appear surprised. "You, you live in Iran?" he stuttered.

"Yes, I've been living there for over fifteen years."

"Are you in the diplomatic corps or in business there? I thought that Iran was very anti-American, and it would not be a pleasant place for an American to live?"

"Well, no. I don't have any problems. I've lived there so long that nobody really bothers me. Most of them probably think I'm Iranian."

With a glance at Patricia McClelland inquired," What about you? How is Elizabeth? Are you still married?"

"Yes. Elizabeth is fine."

The questions flew back and forth as they reminisced and talked of old friends and shared events. McClelland could not get enough news of his old friends and associates.

"How about "EP?" he asked.

"EP" is now a US Senator."

"Gee, I didn't know that."

"Do you see him?"

"Oh, we talk every month or so, and I see him several times a year. We go to a VMI football game or when I'm at the beach we either go up to his place or sometimes when he's at the beach at a cottage he owns there."

"What about Will Sutton?"

"Poor Will, I'm sorry to say he's dead. He committed suicide maybe five or six years ago. His marriage broke up, and he apparently went broke," said Alex, who continued with the grim tale of Sutton.

Finally, McClelland turned to Patricia Diaz and said, "You must pardon us. We've been rude, and this must be very uninteresting for you."

"Oh, no. I enjoy hearing you two reminisce," she fibbed.

Alex looked at his watch. "It's getting late, and we have some meetings tomorrow. But, if you're free I would very much like to have dinner with you tomorrow. I have a dinner engagement, but I can easily cancel it."

"That would be fine. I'd like that too. Are you staying here?"

"No, we came over rather unexpectedly and couldn't get reservations here. We are at the Meurice."

"Well, I am going to be busy most of the day tomorrow. Why don't I pick the two of you up at the Meurice around eight o'clock, and we'll go to dinner. I'll make reservations at Tour d'Argent."

Alex interjected, saying, "I thought it was almost impossible to get reservations there."

"The owner's a friend of mine. I do not think we'll have any problem there. In any event, I'll pick you up at eight. I'll have my car, so we won't have to worry about transportation. As a matter of fact, if the car is still here, it can take you back to the Meurice."

McClelland motioned to one of the men in dark suits who immediately came to him.

"Mousla, is the car still outside?"

"Yes, Mr. McClelland.

"Then have the driver take Ms. Diaz and Mr. Blair back to their hotel."

With that he said goodnight and strode across the lobby followed by three of his four bodyguards.

CHAPTER 15

TUESDAY EVENING

The next day they both slept late.

Alex had breakfast in the grill in the basement and left shortly to meet a college classmate, whose business was headquartered in Paris.

Patricia had breakfast in her room. She then went to the U.S. Embassy, which was practically next door to the hotel, where she reported to Robert Gordon using a secure telephone.

Alex's classmate and friend, Mil Stahovich, operated myriad of businesses from his impressive offices on the Champs Elysees. In fact, Mil did business with Alex's coal company, so it was only natural that Alex would call upon him. Alex had called Mil from the hotel to let him know he was in Paris, and Mil had asked him to come over in the late morning and have lunch with him. Alex was delighted to find Mil in Paris. He hoped to use Mil as his excuse and cover in the event that McClelland or his Iranian associates made an inquiry to determine whether or not Alex was truly in Paris on business or whether he was making the trip just to get close to McClelland. He had decided to approach Mil with a genuine business proposition. He didn't want to take the chance that Mil might inadvertently tell someone he was covering for Alex, and he didn't want to use Mil to cover a covert action without telling Mil what he was doing.

The old friends greeted each other. Alex was impressed. Mil's office was large, luxurious and tasteful. After the usual small talk and inquiries about old friends, Alex explained that he was looking for someone to represent him in selling his coal to European customers. Mil was very interested and said that he would like to set up some meetings between some of his associates and Alex. He then called Philippe Montcalm and arranged for Alex and him to see Philippe in the early afternoon.

Alex thought, *"This is really working out well. If the Iranians ever check to see whether my reasons for being in Paris are truly genuine, they will find that they are genuine. However, if the Iranians ever talk to Mil, and Mil says that Alex did not have an appointment that could make them suspicious.* Alex thought that was too remote a possibility for him to worry about it.

By then it was twelve thirty, and Mil said, "Let's go to lunch." They then left Mil's office and walked down the Champs Elysees to the Explorer's Club.

The club, which was situated in an old mansion, exuded old world charm. Alex always enjoyed his visits there with Mil.

Escape from Iran

The three o'clock afternoon meeting went well. Mil and Alex went to the offices of Layfayette et Fils. Phillipe seemed genuinely interested and said that he would plan to come to the United States after New Year's.

When Alex and Mil left the building in which Lafayette's offices were located, Alex declined Mil's offer of a ride to the Meurice and said that he would prefer to walk back, because he needed the exercise.

Alex returned to the hotel. He wanted to call his office in Richmond, but he noted that because of the time difference it was now 10:00 a.m. in Richmond, which was pretty early for anything, so he decided to wait until later and get some rest before the dinner with McClelland. He called Patricia in her room and told her to meet him in the lobby at 7:25. McClelland was to meet them there at 7:30, and Alex hated being late. He felt it was rude to make someone wait for you.

Promptly at 7:30 McClelland strolled into the lobby of the Maurice, followed discreetly by two of his bodyguards. With a warm smile, he said, "Good evening, Patricia. You look absolutely spectacular in that outfit."

It was true. Patricia did look spectacular.

He turned to Alex and said, "Good evening, Alex. You don't look too bad either. Are you all ready for dinner? Let's go."

The three of them walked through the entrance where a gleaming black Rolls Royce limousine stood awaiting them. Alex noticed the

G. Gray Garland

chauffeur, who was holding open the rear door, had Middle Eastern features and, he also noticed it was the same car that had taken them to the Meurice the night before. It obviously belonged to McClelland. As they pulled away Alex said, "My, but it's nice to have successful friends. Isn't it, Patricia?"

McClelland chuckled, obviously pleased.

The short ride to the restaurant was occupied with small talk.

"Did you have a nice day, Patricia?"

"Yes, I did. I slept in and had breakfast in my room. Then I went over to the Embassy to check on some things for Mr. Blair."

"And you, Alex?" McClelland was obviously enjoying being the host or perhaps he was gently probing.

"Yes, Bob, my day went okay. I had a couple of meetings on a coal deal I am trying to put together with an old friend and classmate.

McClelland, looking very much at home in the plush Rolls, said, "VMI? Do I know him?"

Alex, looking at the sights, casually replied, "No, Mil Stahovich from Harvard Business School. Do you know him?"

"No, I don't think so, but I have heard of him. I'm told he just built a cosmetics plant in Russia. A little risky, if you ask me. The Russians are not easy to deal with. I know."

Alex, continuing to look out of the car window said, "What about your day?"

Escape from Iran

"Oh, the usual. When I come up to Paris, I usually have a pretty full schedule. Incidentally," he said, changing the subject very adeptly and looking at Patricia, "That's Notre Dame we are about to pass. It's very pretty when it's lit up at night."

A few minutes later they arrived at the restaurant. It was very obvious that McClelland was a valued customer. The doorman greeted him by name and escorted them in to the maitre'd, who did everything but kiss McClelland's ring. "Ah, Monsieur McClelland. So good to see you again.. We have missed you."

"Thank you, Jean Pierre. It's good to be back."

They were shown to the best table in the restaurant, a table with a beautiful view overlooking the Seine and the Cathedral of Notre Dame.

"I'm impressed," said Alex. "So am I," replied Patricia.

McClelland beamed with pleasure. He was enjoying his being able to show his importance and influence, and he was enjoying having the opportunity to talk and banter with fellow Americans.

The restaurant was known throughout the world as one of the very best. The meal was superb and lived up to the restaurant's reputation.

The conversation was mostly small talk about the sights of Paris and about old friends of Alex and McClelland

However, Alex detected, or thought he detected, gentle probing with respect to Patricia.

"How long have you worked for Alex?"

"Oh, about two years. I worked at one of the subsidiary companies and then was moved to corporate headquarters."

What a masterful reply, thought Alex. *Howeve,r I hope they can't check that out.*

"Where did you go to school?"

"Hollins," she replied, "Hollins in Roanoke, Virginia. And I later took courses at the University of Mexico."

McClelland's face lit up. "I know Hollins. I went to VMI with Alex. Of course, we were there a few years before your time."

The conversation continued about Hollins, VMI, and VMI cadets dating girls from Hollins. Then the conversation turned to Mexico. Alex did not know whether or not it was true that Patricia had actually attended the University of Mexico. He hoped this would not cause McClelland to be suspicious.

McClelland said, "I spent a lot of time in Mexico." With that the conversation became a three way dialogue on Mexico with Alex recounting the times he had seen McClelland when he had been going to Mexico on business.

Patricia knew her Mexico well. Alex relaxed.

Alex thought it somewhat odd that McClelland made no inquiries about his business career, but was somewhat stunned and taken aback

Escape from Iran

when he was discussing Patricia's duties and McClelland said to Patricia "Did you work for Alex's telephone company?"

"Yes," replied Patricia, "for a short time before being transferred to headquarters."

"*Good answer*," thought Alex. Corporate records had been "adjusted" at the direction of the CIA to reflect this. *How could Bob know that unless he's done some checking, thought Alex. Good Lord! Since last night?*

After dinner McClelland suggested that they go to see the famous can-can dancers. Patricia readily agreed, much to the disappointment of Alex, who was hoping to get McClelland alone. It was well after midnight when the three of them started back to the Meurice.

Alex was disappointed. He had not wanted to probe McClelland with Patricia present for fear that McClelland would be reluctant to talk. And he had had no opportunity to be alone with him. Further and most important of all there had been absolutely no hint of an invitation to visit Bob in Iran.

"When are you going back to the States?" asked Bob.

Alex replied by saying, "Probably, the day after tomorrow. I've done pretty much all I can do here."

The limousine pulled up in front of the Maurice and one of the bodyguards who had been following in a second car opened the door.

"It's been a lovely evening, Mr. McClelland. I thank you so very much."

McClelland interrupted Patricia, "Please call me Bob."

She smiled and gave him a kiss on his cheek. "Thank you, Bob. I hope we get to see you again very soon."

"I do too, Patricia. Alex, it was nice to see you and hear all the news from home. Good luck." He shook hands with both Patricia and Alex, entered the limousine and was whisked away.

Alex felt suddenly very tired and depressed. The mission to Paris had been a failure and by coming over here he had probably blown the PC&R deal.

Patricia, noticing Alex's somber mood, said, "Alex, let's get a nightcap."

"Patricia, I don't think I could look at another drink tonight. On second thought, I'll just have a cup of hot tea."

They went into the bar. She ordered a Rob Roy and he ordered a pot of hot tea.

"Well, Patricia, I think we can write off our trip to Paris."

"I agree that things don't look too good, but I have an idea, Alex."

"What's that?"

"Let's call him tomorrow and tell him that our stay has been extended. W can say we would like to get together with him for dinner tomorrow night or maybe better yet, you call him and tell him your meeting has been cancelled and you are free for lunch and dinner, if he is free."

Escape from Iran

"Well, it's certainly worth a try."

Alex noticed that her hand was on his.

"Alex," she said, "Let's go up and get some rest."

However, Alex thought, *"There is no rest for the weary."*

Alex stayed up very late, until early morning in New York, calling New York, Richmond Philadelphia. He awakened Krantz. Alex explained that they had planned to give the treasurer of PC&R some stock, but in as much as they had not informed him, Alex thought that it would be all right to eliminate him as a shareholder. Alex also said that he thought that some shares were to be issued separately to husband and wife. If instead they were combined and only one certificate was issued jointly to the husband and wife they would be considered as one shareholder instead of two shareholders. Frantz professed not to know whether this would work, but stated that he would look into it and try to get the PC&R deal back on track. Frantz said he thought that they were only two or three shareholders over the requirement for an exemption, and if Alex promised that he would see that at least three shareholders were eliminated, David would agree this could solve the problem. David said he thought that it would work, but he would have to check and get back to Alex. As they ended the call he agreed again with Alex that this would probably work, but Alex thought he probably was still asleep when he said so.

87

Later the next morning Patricia suggested that Alex call Bob McClelland. The crisp female voice that answered the phone said that Mr. McClelland was not in but that she would give him Alex's message. Alex asked that McClelland call him as soon as he had time.

The phone rang while Alex was in the shower. Patricia answered it and called Alex.

"Alex, it's for you. It's Bob."

Alex, still dripping wet, wrapped a towel around his waist and went into the bedroom to answer the phone. Patricia handed him the phone with one hand and with the other hand pulled the towel away with the other.

"Damn it Patricia, give me back that towel."

Bob chuckling said, "What's going on, Alex?"

"Nothing, nothing. We are going to stay over for another day. I wondered if you were free for lunch today." Patricia was now hugging him, and he found it very difficult to continue the conversation. "Bob let me call you back in about an hour."

Bob chuckled, "I understand, I'll be here."

Alex hung up. Patricia said, "See Alex, things aren't all that bad."

CHAPTER 16

WEDNESDAY

"Why don't you have lunch alone with him? I think there's a chance he'll talk more freely if I'm not there," said Patricia buttoning Alex's shirt.

"I agree. If things work out, we can all have dinner together."

Alex called McClelland and they agreed to meet at one o'clock for lunch at Maxim's.

After hanging up the phone, Alex felt pressured and restless. He felt he needed to get out of the hotel and take a long walk. Around ten Alex strolled through the lobby and onto the street. It was a nice day, but the weather felt like rain and was somewhat cool. He returned to his room and retrieved his raincoat. He had plenty of time before his luncheon engagement, so he decided to walk. He always enjoyed walking around Paris. For a few minutes he strolled around Place Vendome, looking into the various shop windows. He saw nothing he wanted to buy for himself or for a gift to take home to Elizabeth.

G. Gray Garland

He strolled past the Ritz Hotel and the U.S. embassy. Seeing the U. S. Embassy, he wondered if he was being followed. He assumed he probably was, but there was no sign of anyone following him. He walked up to Avenue Victor Hugo and window shopped. He went into Holland and Holland and purchased several neckties. They were decorated with hunting scenes, hunters shooting birds and hunters with dogs. He liked to wear these ties when he was in the country at his farm and went to the Rolling Rock Club for dinner or for a party. He paid for them with his American Express card and arranged to have them sent to Ligonier. He lingered a few minutes to examine several shotguns.

As he left Holland and Holland he looked at his watch. It was later than he thought. "I am going to have to get a taxi in order to be on time." Luckily, a taxi was discharging several passengers in front of a nearby store. Alex was able to take it. Notwithstanding his long walk, with a quick taxi ride he arrived at Maxim's about fifteen minutes early. He was about to enter the restaurant when McClelland's big, black Rolls-Royce pulled up to the curb, and before his bodyguards could jump out and open the back door, McClelland opened the back door, leaped out and called, "Hey Alex, wait for me." McClelland was obviously very excited to see his old friend again.

The lunch was excellent and relaxed. McClelland, as usual, seemed to know the maitre d and all of the waiters by name, and they also

Escape from Iran

knew him. About halfway through the entree, Alex said to McClelland, "Bob, if I'm not prying, what the hell do you do in Iran? How can an American function there with the ayatollahs and all of the hatred toward the Americans?"

McClelland looked around the room at the nearby tables and slowly put down his coffee cup, "I have a trading company. I buy armaments and other vital supplies for Iran. Because I am an American and because I have the contacts they need to procure certain crucial items, they have to put up with me."

"Doesn't this put you crosswise with the U.S. government?"

"I suppose so." He hesitated, looked at Alex, and then said, "Well, to tell you the truth, I don't know. I've never done anything to harm the United States government."

"Don't you have any desire to come home?"

"No, not really. There's nothing in the States that I want. I have no family there. Oh, I guess that sometimes I get a little lonely and homesick. But I am afraid that if I did come back, I might get hassled or even put in jail, even though I know that I haven't done anything wrong."

Alex remained quiet, looking down at the table and playing with a spoon.

Suddenly, McClelland quietly blurted out, "Alex, I'm not being honest with you. To tell you the truth I really would like to get out of Iran. I have enough money in Swiss banks to live well for the rest of my life. When I purchased items for the Iranians I always had the person who sold them deposit the commissions for me in one of my Swiss banks. Things are not really as they appear. I am more or less a prisoner." He paused to look around to see if anyone, including his bodyguards might be listening. "They seemed to be enjoying their meal at a back table, not paying any attention to McClelland.

"Sure, I can go around in my private plane. However, the pilots are all from the Iranian Air Force. My bodyguards are really Iranian security people. They would kill me if they thought I was going to defect or do something that they thought was out of line. Sure, I live in a palace full of magnificent furniture and antiques. But what do I really have? It's a very lonely and nerve-racking existence. If I could figure a way to get out of Iran with my life, I would surely do so. Alex, do you think anything could be done?"

Alex was quiet for a moment and then he saidsaid, "Why don't you talk to someone in the U.S. government and see what your status is?"

"Alex, that's not as easy as it sounds. I've thought about it."

"Then why don't you get someone to do it for you?"

McClelland's mood seemed to change. "I don't know anyone, who would or could do that for me." His mood seemed to shift. "Besides, I have a pretty good life in Iran. You should see my homes."

Escape from Iran

"I wish I could, but I'm afraid that I would not be allowed to visit you, even if you invited me."

"No, the Iranians wouldn't hassle you if you came to see me. Where you would be hassled would be in the United States when you got back. The CIA would figure you were up to no good, and they would probably try to pin something on you."

"Well, I wouldn't want that, but I am inclined to believe that they would be happy to have someone go over there. From what I read, they are almost desperate to open up a relationship with Iran."

"Well, just between you and me, there's not much chance of that as long as the Ayatollah Marzai lives." McClelland continued, "Frankly, I'm sort of surprised that the CIA hasn't had the ayatollah assassinated."

"I don't think the CIA can do that sort of thing anymore."

"Fiddlesticks."

"No. Bob, I think that with all the congressional oversight, it's just something they don't do anymore."

McClelland shrugged and pressed on," Well, that may be true but they are still capable of getting someone like the Israelis to do the dirty job for them."

Alex did not answer. A waiter refilled their coffee and discreetly left them alone.

After a period of silence McClelland spoke, "You know Alex, I've been thinking."

93

G. Gray Garland

"Thinking what?"

"You're a lawyer. You know a lot of people. Maybe you could find out whether or not I would have any trouble, if I returned to the United States. I've made plenty of money. I'm thirty-nine almost forty years old. Maybe I should retire while I am ahead of the game. Why don't you check into this for me? What do you think?"

"Sure, I'm a lawyer, but I've never done anything like this. I don't actively practice law. I'm more involved as a business executive." Alex was silent for several moments, and then he said, "Okay, let me see what I can do."

"Good, but I want to pay you a fat fee for this."

Alex was thinking, *"This is going better than I ever have anticipated. Maybe, if I play my cards right I can get the Ayatollah Montarezzi out of Iran and at the same time make a deal for Bob to come home."*

"Bob, don't be insulting. I would never accept a fee for doing this for an old friend. Besides, I'm not sure I can do anything with something like this. If I can arrange something, how would I communicate with you? I don't imagine you would want me to call you on the phone or write you a letter."

"No, I wouldn't want that." Perhaps we'll have to wait until I come again to Paris."

Alex paused and shifted in his seat." No, that won't work either. If I meet you here, having been seen with you as much as I have during

94

this trip, they'll be very suspicious that I am up to something with you. Let's think about it, and maybe we'll have a better solution at dinnertime. You are free for dinner, aren't you?"

"Yes, of course. What about Patricia?" replied McClelland.

"We'll just tell her we want to talk alone for a few minutes, or we'll excuse ourselves and go to the men's room."

Alex folded his napkin. "Okay, it's already close to three o'clock. I've got a couple of calls to make. We better get going."

"Do you want a lift back to the hotel?"

"No thanks, I think I would like to walk. I don't ever get any exercise in Paris, and I do nothing but eat."

"Allright, I'll pick you and Patricia up at the Meurice at about eight. Okay?"

"Yes, that will be fine."

Upon his return Alex related the events of his luncheon to Patricia. She was jubilant.

That night the three of them had dinner at Tour d'Argent. The conversation was pleasant and light and no mention was made of Alex's conversation with McClelland. The only clue that McClelland remembered the luncheon conversation came after dinner when his Rolls dropped them off at the Maurice. McClelland got out of the car to say goodbye. Patricia kissed him on the cheek and thanked him for

G. Gray Garland

a lovely evening. He squeezed Alex's arm and said, "It's been great being with you, you'll hear from me."

In another instant the Rolls Royce was disappearing down the street followed by his escort car of bodyguards.

Alex said, "Patricia, I feel like a nightcap, how about you?"

Patricia's face lit up and she said with a coy smile, "Yes, I do. Why don't we have them sent up to your room?"

CHAPTER 17

WEDNESDAY A WEEK LATER

A large and very dusty black Mercedes 600 sedan followed by an equally dusty Land Rover pulled into the courtyard. Two soldiers from the Land Rover jumped out immediately, and one ran up and opened the rear passenger door of the big sedan. An Iranian general in full uniform descended from the car and immediately went into the house, ignoring the salutes of the two soldiers guarding the door of the house, who recognized the Chief of Intelligence of Iran.

The white washed walls of the Ayatollah's residence were bare. The furniture was simple, mostly comfortable, heavily cushioned easy chairs with small, low tables beside each chair. Without speaking, the older Ayatollah motioned for the General to sit in the empty chair next to him. As if on cue a waiter in a white jacket entered the room, poured steaming tea into the teacup on the low table by each occupant and retired from the room. The three men sitting in the heavily cushioned easy chairs sipped in silence.

G. Gray Garland

Finally, Majid, the one in uniform, spoke in Farsi. "I understand that McClelland has your permission to invite an American to come here."

The older of the two robed men took a sip of his tea and spoke for the first time. "Yes, that is true. I gave him permission to do so. After all he has done so much for us. I did not feel I could deny his request. Besides, McClelland says that his friend, Blair, may be able to help us to obtain some very hard to find metals. Allah knows, we need help in getting these metals for our program."

Pausing only to place his cup on the low table before his chair, the Chief of Intelligence, spoke again "I have checked into Blair. I am told what McClelland has told you is true. Blair did attend college with McClelland. He was in the American Marines with him during Desert Storm. However, Blair is a wealthy industrialist in the United States, and from what I can gather, he is an avowed capitalist. It makes no sense for him get involved with us. He is a man of wealth and position in his own country. Why would he come here and risk this?"

The older Ayatollah replied, "You know the Americans. They'll do anything for money. They would sell their souls. They have no scruples when it comes to money. However, I am concerned, but what can I do? I told McClelland he could invite Mr. Blair to come here. I cannot go back on my word." The Ayatollah's statement hung in silence for a

Escape from Iran

few moments. Then the older man spoke again, "If Blair comes, you will have to watch him carefully."

Majid placed his cup on the table and looking the older man in the eye for what seemed like a long moment replied, "Let me see what I can do to solve your problem."

"What do you have in mind?"

The three stopped sipping their tea for a few more moments and looked at Majid. There was silence. For several moments no one said a word. Then Majid quietly said, "Perhaps Mr. Blair will never come to Iran."

The senior Ayatollah looked at Majid and answered, "Perhaps you are correct, Majid. I continue to be blessed by having you as my Chief of Intelligence and Security. What you say makes sense. However, I have given my word. I cannot go back on it with McClelland. He is too valuable to us." He shrugged. "Perhaps it can be arranged so that Mr. Blair will never come to Iran. As always, I thank you for coming to see me. "

The meeting was obviously over. Majid knew he was dismissed. He stood up, bowed, and quickly exited the building. Within minutes he was sprawled in the back seat of his limousine, contemplating what his next move should be. *Blair should not be allowed to come to Iran. Something is not right. McClelland has never had anyone like Blair come to visit him. He's always done his business by visiting them or by telephone.*

Maybe he really wants to have his old friend come for a visit. I don't think so. In any event I don't think we should take that chance.

As soon as the Chief of Intelligence returned to his office in Tehran he summoned his chief of foreign intelligence. He told him of his meeting with the Ayatollah. "McClelland is too valuable to us for us to have a confrontation with him. However, the Ayatollah and I do not like having American friends visit him here. In the past we have discouraged this in an indirect way by making it difficult for Americans to obtain a visa. However, we cannot do this, since McClelland himself has obtained permission from the Ayatollah himself."

"It would be appropriate, if an accident could be arranged for Mr. Blair. By doing this we would discourage McClelland's having visitors, but we would not be having a direct confrontation with him. He could never prove that we had anything to do with the accident, but he is smart enough to think perhaps we did. Do you think you can arrange something like this?"

"Yes, General, I am certain I can arrange to take care of the problem. It will never be something connected to us."

CHAPTER 18

General Majid Heikal al-Sadat. Iran's Chief of Intelligence, was a graduate of Harvard University, and an avowed Marxist, and he hated the United States and all Americans with a passion.

While in his final year of the Iranian equivalent of high school he won a Rockwood Scholarship to Harvard. He was one of only three throughout the entire world to win such a scholarship, and he was the first one from Iran to ever have won a scholarship from Iran.

During his first few months in the United States he was too filled with the joy of his accomplishment in obtaining the Rockwood Scholarship to be lonely. He was completely awed by the United States, its skyscrapers, the masses of shiny new automobiles, and the ordinary appliances, such as washing machines, televisions etc. Also his days were busy. There were many meetings for new students and a number of receptions for foreign students.

He could not get over the modern conveniences of the Americans. It was so different from his village in Iran. He was

G. Gray Garland

enamored with the skyscrapers taller than any buildings he had ever dreamed of, streets clogged with magnificent automobiles, women who walked the streets in magnificent clothes showing their faces and limbs, and above all modern plumbing. In his home they had neither running water nor plumbing. He reveled in taking hot showers. His room in the dormitory was magnificent, although he found his roommate somewhat strange and uncommunicative.

After a few months the novelty wore off and he was very lonely.

His roommate Jim Cotter was from Brookline, and he spent more time at home than in their dormitory room. He was considerate and polite, but he made no effort to really befriend Majid. Majid's English was, in fact, excellent, but he lacked the confidence to speak English, a language foreign to him. Therefore he seldom, if ever, initiated a conversation. However, he understood perfectly what was said around him.

He studied hard and achieved excellent grades, but he was very lonely for companionship. While the Rockwood Scholarship paid his tuition and all of his college expenses, the spending money that it gave to him was barely enough to subsist on. On weekends and holidays he would take long walks or occasionally indulge himself with a subway or bus ride.

Escape from Iran

During his sophomore year he visited the Boston Museum of Fine Arts and was fascinated with the beautiful paintings that hung on its walls.

He found out that there were free lectures at the museum, and whenever he could, he attended these lectures. In his spare time he would often go to the Harvard Fine Arts Library or the Boston Public Library to read about the artists and their paintings.

Early in his junior year he was attending a lecture on the life and paintings of Claude Monet, when he saw Susan Higgins, a Radcliff student who sat beside him in his English literature course. Susan was like the other students. They might say 'Hello' when they saw him, but they never made any real attempt to befriend him. He longed to be asked to go for a cup of coffee or be invited to drink a beer, even though he did not touch alcoholic beverages.

After the lecture there was the usual coffee hour during which the attendees could meet and talk with the lecturer. Majid enjoyed these. He would have his coffee, and he loved the wonderful little cakes. He would stand near the lecturer and listen to the conversations, but he was too shy to participate in the conversations. However, standing with the group surrounding the lecturer gave him a feeling of belonging.

G. Gray Garland

He was standing at the side table pouring himself a cup of coffee when Susan came up and said, "Majid, I'm surprised to see you here I did not know that you were interested in art."

"Oh yes. I am very interested. I come here often for all the lectures."

"What did you think of the lecture?" asked Susan, and with that their friendship was born.

CHAPTER 19

Susan was stunning, a real American beauty, a natural blonde, five foot eight inches tall with a striking figure. She could easily have been a movie star. To Majid she was the most beautiful and the most intelligent human being he had ever met.

Simply stated he was head over heels in love with her.

After that first night at the museum, Majid and Susan found they had much in common. Majid had become quite knowledgeable about art, which was truly Susan's great interest. Also they both were voracious readers, which gave them much to talk about.

Their dates, if you could call them that, consisted mainly of lingering over tea or Coca-Colas at the college snack shop. Majid longed to take Susan to dinner, but he simply did not have the money to do so. Susan was a day student, so the only time Majid saw her in the evenings was when they would meet at the museum for a lecture. After the lecture they would linger over coffee and cakes. Then she would return to her home and he to his lonely dormitory room. Jim Cotter, his roommate, seldom used the room. Majid presumed he went home most nights to his parents' home in Brookline.

On the last day of classes before the Thanksgiving break Susan said to Majid, "My family would love to have you come to our home for Thanksgiving dinner."

Majid readily accepted.

Thanksgiving dinner was unbelievable. When Majid arrived at the large home on Beacon Hill, he first thought that they must be having dinner at a hotel or a club. He was overwhelmed by the size of Susan's home. He rang the doorbell and was greeted by a tall, distinguished white haired man wearing a white coat and black bow tie.

This must be Susan's father", he thought, but before he could speak, the tall man bowed slightly and said, "Good evening sir. You must be Mr. Heikal. I am Rollitt, the Higgins' butler. Let me have your coat. Everyone is in the library. Let me show you the way."

Rollitt opened the double doors, and they entered a large but cozy, paneled library. Susan spotted Majid and immediately detached herself from a group standing near the fireplace and came across the room to greet him.

Susan was wearing a plain white blouse and a long Scotch-plaid skirt. She was the most beautiful thing Majid had ever seen. She took his hand in hers and led him around the room introducing him to

Escape from Iran

everyone "This is my friend, Majid, from Iran," she said to each of them, as she introduced him.

They all greeted him warmly. Susan's mother seemed particularly warm and friendly. "Welcome to our home, Mr. Heikal," she said.

Majid had never seen such elegant and handsome people. They were truly "The beautiful people" he had read about in the newspapers. The older men were in evening clothes, but some of the younger men were in sports coats and slacks, so Majid did not feel out of place.

In fact, he was so thrilled at Susan's holding his hand that he could hardly contain himself. She had never held his hand before, and to do this in her parents' home was almost more than he could bear.

Her mother and father and all of the guests were so friendly that for the first time since he arrived in the United States some two years ago he felt as it he finally belonged.

Thus began many visits to the Higgins home.

CHAPTER 20

During the balance of the school year Majid continued to see Susan often. They continued to meet between classes for coffee and conversation, and they continued to attend the lectures at the Boston Museum. After most of the lectures they would have coffee in the museum cafeteria and then part company, Susan to her home in a taxi and Majid to his dorm by subway or bus.

One night in December it was very cold and snowy. After the lecture Susan said, "Majid, the weather is really bad. I think we had better skip our coffee tonight. I'll give you a ride home . Rollitt is going to meet me out front. "

When they exited the museum Susan exclaimed, "There he is," pointing to a Jeep Station Wagon with the name "Highpointe" written on its front door panel. Rollitt, who had parked in front of the door, immediately spotted them and got out of the car to open the doors for them.

"Good evening, Miss Susan. Good evening, Mr. Majid."

Escape from Iran

With Susan and Majid in the backseat, Rollitt deftly maneuvered the car into the stream of traffic. When they arrived at Majid's dorm, Susan squeezed his hand and said, "Thank you for going with me Majid. It's always so nice to be with you."

Majid replied, "Susan, I do enjoy being with you. I"

However, before he could finish Rollitt was holding open the rear door. Majid got out of the car. All he could now say was, "Good night, Susan."

Susan smiled warmly and replied, "Good night, Majid"

Majid could not sleep that night. He kept thinking, *She likes me. She likes me.*

During the Christmas break he only saw Susan three times. They went to a lecture at the museum, he went to her home for Christmas dinner, and they met once at the Harvard Fine Arts Library. Majid was disappointed, and lonely, but he thought he understood. *Christmas is a big family holiday in America. Everyone spends a lot of time with his family.*

After the Christmas break, they resumed their regular routine.

Once or twice he held her hand, but that was about it.

He wanted so much to tell her how much he was in love with her, but he was too shy to say anything. In any event, how could he marry such a rich girl? He had no job and no money. He could hardly take her to dinner much less support her.

G. Gray Garland

One day as Spring Break approached, Susan said "This year we are going to our home in Maine for Spring Break. My family would like to know if you would like to come with us. You can drive up with my father. Mother and I are going up early to get the house in order. No one has used it since last September."

CHAPTER 21

On Thursday afternoon, as arranged, Susan's father, Myles Higgins, picked up Majid at the house on Beacon Hill for the drive to Highpointe.

He told Majid that Rollitt had driven Mrs. Higgins and Susan to Maine in the Jeep Station Wagon several days earlier. They had arrived in good shape and were waiting for Mr. Higgins and Majid.

Even if you did not know Myles Higgins's background, he was a very impressive individual. He was tall and slender, well groomed, and with the patrician look of a Boston bank president, which, of course, he was.

He deftly maneuvered the big Cadillac Fleetwood through Boston's traffic, all the while putting Majid at his ease. "Have I mentioned to you the girls got up to Highpointe all right? Sometimes it's tricky this time of the year. We have a lot of snow, and the roads aren't too good."

Majid, impressed by the car and trying to make conversation, exclaimed, "This is certainly a nice automobile."

G. Gray Garland

"Yes, It is. This is a very quiet car. It is a Cadillac. We have been buying Cadillacs for many years." Higgins continued to make the conversation flow easily, putting Majid at ease. Majid found that he was very comfortable talking with Mr. Higgins.

"Susan tells me you are very interested in art. Have you been to the Higgins Wing at the museum? My grandfather gave it to the museum. Our foundation still supports it. You will love Maine, especially, if we have decent weather. It's a little tricky this time of the year. We have been going to Hobe Sound for spring vacations, but my sister, Martha Updyke-you know her, you met her at our house- has not been well, so we gave her the house in Florida for the winter. It will be nice for her to recoup in the sunshine. She really needs peace and quiet, so we decided not to go down this year. Too much confusion for her. Anyway, it should be fun to go to Highpointe in March. We seldom have been up there in cold weather, but when we did go, it has always been relaxing and fun."

Majid was flattered. *He is really interested in me. I think he is trying to find out what sort of husband I would be for his daughter.*

Mr. Higgins continued. "What are you majoring in? I know that you take a course in English literature with Susan."

"I am taking a course leading to a BA in Economics."

Escape from Iran

Not missing a beat as he gunned the Cadillac and passed a large truck, Mr. Higgins continued. "What do you want to do when you finish Harvard?"

"I shall likely go back to Iran where I shall probably teach or go to work for the government. There are not too many jobs in private business, and I don't have enough money to start my own business, at least not yet."

"What are you planning to do during your summer vacation?"

"I really don't know, sir. I may go to summer school, if my scholarship permits it. You know I am here on a Rockwood Scholarship."

"Majid, would you like to come to work for my bank this summer?"

Majid could not believe what he was hearing. His spirits soared only to fall back somewhat when he replied. "I certainly would like to, but I don't believe I can. I don't have a green card."

"Oh, don't worry about that. If you would like to come to work for the bank, I can take care of that."

"Yes, I would like very much to work for your bank."

"Good, I think the experience would be very helpful for your career. If you go back to Iran, you may be able to get a good job in a bank."

Majid was elated. *Mr. Higgins had said "If". He must be planning for me to stay here.*

The Maine house was beautiful. It was a large sprawling stone and frame house on a high promontory of land that looked out over the ocean on one side and a small inlet on the other side.

When they arrived Mrs. Higgins gave him a kiss on his cheek. "Welcome, Majid. Welcome to Highpointe."

The first two days were pure heaven to Majid. It was cold and rainy, but Majid enjoyed putting on heavy clothes, walking with Susan along the beach, and returning to drink hot chocolate by the roaring fire, which was always kept lighted in the large fireplace in the living room. He wanted so much to take Susan in his arms and to hug and kiss her. He knew she loved him. She held his hand sometimes when they walked on the beach.

On Friday afternoon other guests began to arrive for the weekend. The idyll of being alone with Susan ended when an older couple, friends of the Higgins family, arrived in mid afternoon. Shortly afterwards they were followed by Susan's brother, George, and his roommate Armistead Diaz. They were flying to Canada for a ski trip in Diaz's private plane, but they had decided to land and spend the night at Highpointe, because they said the weather to the north was too poor for flying.

CHAPTER 22

The following summer Majid went to work for Boston Bank and Trust Company, generally known throughout the financial world as "BB&T". He started in the banks trainee program and was amazed at how much money he made as a trainee. He seldom saw Mr. Higgins at the bank, but he did visit Highpointe twice during the summer. In between visits he wrote regular letters to Susan who spent the summer away from Boston. The letters were friendly and stilted, not amorous. He was very shy in expressing his feelings. Susan only wrote back twice during the summer. Her two letters were newsy, not romantic. However, she did sign both of his letters "With love," which absolutely thrilled Majid.

After his last visit to Highpointe in mid August he was determined he was going to tell Susan of his love for her He had saved most of the money he had made during the summer. He would take her to a nice restaurant and have a romantic candlelight dinner. Then he would

G. Gray Garland

tell her of his love for her. He had never been happier. Coming to the United States of America was the best thing that had ever happened to him.

CHAPTER 23

Majid's glorious summer was over. September had at last come to Boston. Labor Day was next Monday. The days were sunny and warm. The nights were cool with a touch of fall in the air. All Majid could think about was that Susan would soon return from Highpointee, and he could tell her of his love for her. He had finished his summer job at the bank, and he had saved a considerable sum of money, at least in his estimation. As soon as Susan returned, he would profess his love for her.

He had been to Highpointe only twice during the summer. It was difficult for Majid to get to Highpointe, unless Mr. Higgins, who commuted from Boston to Highpointe and back to Boston on a regular basis, offered him a ride. Even then it was difficult. Majid had to be back at the bank on Monday, and Mr. Higgins often decided to stay over for a day or two, which left Majid in an embarrassing position. He felt that he was welcome at Highpointe, but he had only received two invitations. There were always numerous guests at Highpointe,

G. Gray Garland

both young and old, when he was there. The older guests seemed to accept him readily. The younger ones more or less tolerated him. He rarely had any time to be alone with Susan. They had taken several walks on the beach and he had held her hand, but that was about all that had happened. He was too shy to write a love letter, although he had always signed his letters "With love." It did not bother him at that time that he had not received any replies to his letters, since he was usually looking forward to making a visit to see her at Highpointe.

Classes at Harvard began, and Majid looked forward to seeing Susan. He was sure she would now be back from Highpointe. He had called her home on Beacon Hill several times. Rollitt, who answered the phone, always seemed happy to hear from Majid, but all he would say was, "Miss Susan is still out-of-town." Majid was concerned that he had not heard from Susan, but deep in his heart he knew that Susan's loved him. Several more weeks went by, and there was still no word from Susan. Majid decided to he must overcome his shyness and go to Beacon Hill to see what was happening. He walked from his dormitory room all the way to Susan's house on Beacon Hill. When he arrived at the house he paced up-and-down outside on the street before he got up enough courage to go up the steps and ring the doorbell.

Much to his great surprise, it was not Rollitt who opened the door, but his beloved Susan. She was gushing and radiant. He had never

Escape from Iran

seen her so happy. "Oh, Majid, I am so happy to see you. Come in. Come in. I have wonderful news to tell you."

Majid, still knowing that Susan loved him, was absolutely stunned when she said, "I'm engaged. I am going to be married in June. I am so happy. It's my brother's roommate at Yale. I think you met him at Highpointe. You must come to the wedding." She babbled on, but Majid did not hear or absorb any of the words. All he knew was that his world had ended. He did not remember what he did or what he said. Somehow he got out of Susan's house. He did not even remember the long, lonely walk back to his lonely dormitory room. He stopped going to classes. He stayed in his room most of the time. He seldom had anything to eat. He was completely devastated. All he could think about was Susan and what she had done to him. After a while his depression began to turn to hate, intense hate, hate for Susan, hate for Harvard, hate for everything American. It was then he decided to leave America immediately after graduation and return to Iran. He could not disgrace his country and leave without graduating, but he was a very, very embittered Iranian.

CHAPTER 24

Several weeks had passed since Alex had returned from France and reported to Robert Gordon about his conversations with McClelland. He emphasized to Gordon, that if it was possible to persuade him to come back to the United States that it would be necessary for McClelland to be guaranteed immunity from prosecution. Alex said he would be willing to go to Iran to tell McClelland about the immunity, but that would be it, but he did not want to be involved beyond delivering the message. He knew McClelland would not trust anyone else to tell him about the immunity. Alex further said that he would want to examine any documents pertaining to McClelland's immunity to ascertain McClelland would have no problems when he returned to the United States.

Since talking to Gordon, Alex had heard nothing more about Iran. Now his mind was on his own businesses and Iran was much in the background. The acquisition of PC&R once more appeared to be on track. The financial details had been settled. It was now a matter

Escape from Iran

of the lawyers working out the intricate details and filing the required documents with the various government agencies. The Scott-Rodino approvals could take up to another ninety days.

The holder of a two percent interest in PC&R had changed his mind and did not wish to sell his shares. Lawyers were researching Delaware law with respect to a so-called "squeeze-out" merger. It appeared that this could be done so long as the dissenting shareholder was paid an amount equal to the market value of his shares.

Patricia had returned to Washington. This worried Alex, who feared that the Iranians would become suspicious if they checked on her and found out she did not actually work for his company. She had been put on the payroll of one of Alex's companies, and the telephone operators had been instructed to say she was away should anyone call to inquire about her. Yet Alex worried. A clever professional could easily see through this. He did talk to Patricia every week or so, but the conversations for the most part related to a phony business deal which the CIA had dreamed up as a front in case anyone should tap Alex's phones.

Alex had not seen Patricia since their trip to France.

In mid-December, Robert Gordon called and requested that Alex and Patricia return to the Virginia estate for further indoctrination and training. The indoctrination rehashed some of what Alex had been told on his first visit, but a great deal of time was devoted to his pending mission and going over his metals business with Gordon and the other trainers helping to instruct him how he should answer possible questions from the Iranians about selling metals to them in spite of the sanctions prohibiting such sales. Gordon said he had been assured that Alex and his company would be given immunity from U.S. sanctions, if it was felt necessary to actually sell some of these metals to the Iranians.

Alex was in no hurry with the mission. It seemed to be expanding beyond his control. It made him very apprehensive. He could not help wondering why he was going through all this training?

They even played a game in which Robert Gordon asked questions and Alex answered them. Patricia listened with silent attention, not missing a word. Finally Gordon was satisfied, and they switched to reviewing maps of Iran and the adjoining countries and assessing possible escape routes and hiding places. They were told to try to go to a certain jewelry shop in Tehran where they might be able to pick up radios and other items, including guns, which the CIA was afraid to have them to take to Iran with them. This really scared Alex.

These training sessions were very interesting to Alex. However, what he really enjoyed were the several sessions devoted to firearms. Alex liked guns, and he enjoyed these courses. Sessions were devoted to fast draw, firing at moving targets, and firing off balance. Although he owned a Sig Sauer semi automatic pistol, which he liked to shoot, he found that he did very well shooting the pistols with which he practiced.

Escape from Iran

After three or four sessions with the excellent CIA instructors Alex began to hit the targets consistently. And in an exercise where Alex was covered by the gun of an adversary, he could simultaneously fall, draw his pistol from the holster, and fire a shot into the heart of his adversary with one quick motion. It all seemed so easy in training. He wondered if he would be able to do this, if he had to under actual conditions. He hoped he would not have to find out.

Other sessions included map reading, learning some basic words in Farsi and reading highway and street signs in Farsi and the use of several types of two-way radios that might be available for his use in Iran. In fact, even though the sessions were necessarily brief, Alex was impressed.

Very little had been left to chance. He had even been issued heavy shoes for hiking and special clothing that would keep him warm should he have to stay outdoors for any length of time. These had a number of secret pockets. He noted that the clothing had labels that claimed the clothes had come from LL. Bean and other well-known mail order houses where Alex would likely have bought such garments.

They even spent several hours one afternoon learning to drive various types of trucks and cars that might be encountered in Iran.

That night when Alex went to bed, he suddenly started to sweat when he wondered why he was going through all of this training, learning to shoot, learning about escape routes, etc. He had been led to believe that all he had to do was to go to Iran and tell Bob that he could obtain the immunity that would let him come home. *I never agreed to be involved in helping Bob to escape from Iran, all I ever agreed to do was to tell Bob that I had arranged for his immunity. The rest should be up to the CIA, not up to me. Why are they giving me all of this training? I feel like I'm about to go over Niagara Falls in a barrel, and I can't get out before it goes over the Falls."*

Alex did not sleep too well that night.

CHAPTER 25

JANUARY

The Christmas season came and went. It happened during the second week in January. Alex was in New York at a dinner party in honor of the Ambassador to the United Nations from India. The party was held by an American friend of Alex's at his east side apartment, which commanded a lovely view of New York.

Although it was quite cold outside, Alex stepped out onto a veranda for a breath of fresh air. A moment or so later he was joined by Walter Butz, the New York representative of a major Swiss bank. Alex had known Butz for a number of years. In fact, Butz had helped Alex to finance one of his major acquisitions.

"Lovely evening, Walter."

"Yes, but it's a little chilly to be out here very long. Alex. I wanted to get you alone. I didn't want to call you on the telephone. I have a message for you from your friend in Iran. He says it will be safe for you to come over. He is telling the Iranians that he may be able to do business with you because of his long-standing friendship with you. He has told them you are a major producer of special metals, which I know is true, and that you may be able to get some of these metals for Iran. He said to tell you this, so that you would understand his letter, which you will receive once he knows that you have been given this message."

"Walter, how in the world..."

Walter stopped lighting his cigarette and again interrupted Alex,

"Alex, I have delivered the message. I will repeat it, if you desire, but don't stretch our friendship by asking me any questions. I shall not answer them. Changing the subject, I have a business proposition that you might be interested in. It involves the purchase of a small bank in Hong Kong. If you're interested, let's have lunch tomorrow. Shall I call you?"

"No, Walter, why don't we just meet at the Racquet Club. Is twelve fifteen okay?"

"Yes, that will be fine."

The two men returned to the party.

Several days later Alex received the letter from McClelland by messenger, inviting him to visit him in Iran and stating that it had been cleared with the Iranian government. He and anyone he might like to accompany him could obtain a visa at the Iranian embassy for the UN in New York.

Escape from Iran

When Alex returned to his apartment from his office on Park Avenue, he called Patricia in Washington. During the conversation he mentioned that there was a good chance that his coal company would be getting an order to sell coal to Spain. When she asked where in Spain, he answered he thought it was Barcelona. "Barcelona" was the code word to let her know that he had heard from McClelland.

CHAPTER 26

JANUARY 1984

When Robert Gordon informed the Director of Alex's invitation from McClelland he immediately made an appointment with the Attorney General to discuss immunity for McClelland. Instead of an expected appointment with the Attorney General at the Department of Justice, Cabot was told the report to the White House the following morning at 11:30 a.m. He was very nervous and apprehensive as he rode into Washington. He had requested a meeting with the Attorney General at his office to discuss obtaining immunity for McClelland, but instead he had received a request, really an order, to report to the White House at 11:30 a.m. on Thursday. He did not like or trust Bill Ashman, the Attorney General. He felt Ashman was extremely arrogant and ambitious. Ashman was a close friend and confidante of the President, and it was rumored that Ashman did the President's dirty work. Ashman and the President went back a long ways. He had been Attorney General of Oklahoma when the President was Governor

Escape from Iran

of California, and they had become friends over a problem Ashman supported for him. He also wondered why he was being asked to meet at the White House. Also the time, 1130 AM, bothered him. He knew that the President usually had lunch with one of the members of his cabinet on Thursday, and he had not been invited for lunch, as far as he knew.

Upon his arrival to his surprise he was not ushered into the Oval Office, but told to report to an office in the old State Department building next door to the White House. A Secret Service Agent, whom he had never seen before, said, "Follow me!" This also puzzled Cabot inasmuch as he knew most of the Secret Service agents at the White House, at least by face. if not my name, since he made almost daily visits to brief the President. He was led through a maze of corridors and stairways to the tunnel, which connected the White House to the old State Department Building. Then they took an elevator to the third floor. He would never have known the President was there, except for two Secret Service agents standing by a door at the end of the hall. One of the agents, whom Cabot knew from prior visits, gave him a smile and a wink as he knocked on the door and announced the Director's arrival. The agent then motioned Cabot to enter. The office was typical of an old fashioned office with its high ceilings, dark wood paneling, old lighting fixtures and even old sectional bookcases with glass doors. The office was bare, except for a large desk, a dark red leather couch and a number of matching side chairs. The walls were a nondescript color and had no paintings or lithographs hanging anywhere. *"It's almost eerie,"* thought Cabot.

The President and the Attorney General were seated when Cabot entered. The President rose from his chair behind the large desk and said, "John, thank you for coming."

The Attorney General remained seated and merely nodded. The President started to say something, but the Attorney General interrupted him and said, "Director, your request is stupid. McClelland is a traitor. For us to grant him immunity would be political suicide."

Before the Attorney General could continue, the President intervened,

"John, I think your idea has a lot of merit, but we are approaching an election year and the press would certainly misinterpret it. We just cannot do it. Bill and I appreciate your coming to see us. You will just have to figure out something else."

Cabot responded, "Mr. President, while I understand the political implications of what you are saying, I'm not concerned for McClelland. He is a traitor, but we're putting Mr. Blair in a very bad position. We are sending him to Iran and taking away his reason for going. We are putting him in a very dangerous position. What can I tell him?"

The President sat down, "John, this mission is too important for our national security for us to abort it. I want you to proceed with it.

Now if you will excuse us, the Attorney General and I have a number of other things to discuss."

With that the Director of the CIA was summarily dismissed. Cabot was ushered out of the office and back to the White House where his black Mercury Marquis sedan and was waiting for him as usual. He startled his driver by climbing into the back seat. He was in a daze. He wanted to think, and so he thought. "*The President, as usual, could give you an answer without giving you an answer. He had clearly said, "John, I want you to proceed." Yet, they had more or less said that McClelland would not be granted immunity. And the office where we met. If I was ever questioned, how could I answer a question like "Where did you meet to discuss this matter?" No one would believe me. It would be like saying we met in a bar on Mass Avenue. What can I do?"*

They drove in silence.

An hour later Cabot entered his office at CIA headquarters and told his secretary to summon Samson and Hogan for a meeting in his conference room. When they arrived they both simultaneously said, "Did you obtain immunity for McClelland?"

The Director merely answered, "The President has authorized us to proceed."

He turned to Sampson and said, "John, you will have the necessary papers prepared granting McClelland immunity. I will have the Attorney General, execute them within the next few days."

He hoped that they would not question him further. It bothered him not to be forthright with his close associates. National security, or perhaps the President, had demanded that he proceed with the mission. However, it was done in a manner that the President and Ashman could deny they authorized it. *In fact, they could say they denied my request for immunity for McClelland, and that I proceeded on my own. If this plan screws up, I'm the one in the soup.*

Hogan stared momentarily at the Director and thought, *Something isn't quite right. I don't know what. Probably my imagination.* He shrugged and said, "I'll get hold of Robert Gordon immediately, so that he may inform Blair that everything is set to go."

Cabot did not contradict Hogan. He quickly ended the meeting by announcing, "Gentleman, thanks, That will be all."

He quickly rose from the conference table and went into his private office, closing the door behind him. He opened the bar in the credenza opposite his desk and made himself a strong scotch, not even stopping to get any ice or water from the refrigerator in the bar. He noticed his hand was shaking. He took a large swig of the scotch and slumped into his desk chair.

CHAPTER 27

JANUARY 1984

Upon learning of the invitation to Iran, Robert Gordon dispatched Patricia to New York. He felt that it would look better if Alex and Patricia went together to obtain their visas at the Iranian Embassy for the United Nations in New York City.

Patricia left Washington on the 9:00 am shuttle and arrived at Alex's offices around eleven thirty. Alex felt that the Iranian visa office would probably be closed at lunchtime, so they decided to grab a quick lunch at a restaurant near the office on 56th Street. Alex said, "Let's walk to the restaurant. It's only a few blocks, and I really need some exercise."

"That's fine by me," said Patricia.

As they walked through the outer office he said to his secretary, "Please have Walter meet us at the restaurant near the apartment on 56th Street."

Alex and Patricia took the elevator from the fortieth floor and walked out onto Park Avenue. Walter was waiting with the car.

"Walter, how about meeting us in about forty-five minutes over at the restaurant on the corner of 56th, across from the apartment?"

Walter smiled and replied, "I know, they just called me from upstairs."

They walked the few blocks down Park Avenue and over 56th Street to the restaurant. Once inside they found a table in the back, sat down and ordered their lunches.

Alex looked around the restaurant to see whether or not he felt it was safe to talk about their proposed project. Most of the patrons appeared to be of foreign extraction. In fact, Alex thought, *I am getting paranoid. Most of the people in New York appear to be foreigners. He decided they better stick to small talk.* Caution was the best policy.

The restaurant was more like a delicatessen. Stools at the counter and booths without table clothes. Because of its convenience to his apartment across the street and its quick service, Alex ate there frequently. They sat in a booth in the back with Patricia facing the front door and Alex facing the rear.

Suddenly, Alex felt a tremendous tension in the air. Patricia's eyes widened as she yelled, "Get down, Alex. Get down!"

Alex ducked. Out of the corner of his eye, he saw Patricia falling out of the booth to her right while at the same time firing a black, automatic pistol that had suddenly appeared in her hand. Alex looked up. The place was in total confusion. Patrons were scrambling for cover.

Escape from Iran

One man in a dark overcoat lay face up. Blood was beginning to spurt up from his forehead. He had been shot between the eyes. Beside him lay a .22 caliber automatic target pistol.

"Alex, is there a back door? Let's get out of here quickly!"

A shaken Alex replied, "Yes, follow me."

As he got up to run for the door, he noticed a man with Middle Eastern features in a dark coat, standing near the front door. The coat was unbuttoned and the man was raising an Uzi machine gun, which had been hanging on a strap from his right shoulder.

Alex screamed, "There's another one!" simultaneously pushing Patricia back onto the floor. The Uzi roared. There was the additional noise of glass shattering as bullets from the machine gun smashed the mirrors behind their booth. Patricia fired twice in the direction of the assailant. Then she grabbed Alex's hand, and they scrambled for the back door.

The man with the machine gun had ducked Patricia's shots and now seemed reluctant to follow them. Maybe Patricia had hit him. Or maybe there were too many people between him and his prey, if Alex and Patricia were the prey.

They reached the curb. Walter and the car were waiting.

They ran to the car shouting to Walter, "Let's get out of here fast. Someone's shooting at us."

By the time they opened the backdoor of the limousine, Walter had the big car moving forward. Alex and Patricia fell into the car. Alex looked back. It did not appear that they were being followed. He turned to Patricia. She was calmly loading a fresh clip into her automatic pistol. The big limousine roared down East 56th Street. Alex and Patricia glanced out of the back window again to see if they were being followed. There were several cars moving behind them but none appeared to be following them. The traffic light at 1st Avenue was red. Walter slowed down. There was a slight break in the traffic. He floored the accelerator and gunned the limo through the red light. At Sutton Place he wheeled left. If anyone was following they would probably be lost now. As they crossed 57th Street going north on Sutton Place two blue and white New York City police cars with lights flashing and sirens screaming passed them moving rapidly in the direction of the restaurant.

It had all happened so fast that neither Alex nor Patricia had had any time to think about the events. Now the shock of it was beginning to sink in. Alex thought, *My God, someone is trying to kill us.* His stomach began to knot up.

Walter, a former police sergeant, said, "Where do you want me to go?"

Patricia said, "Let's stop at a phone booth. I'm afraid to use the car phone."

Escape from Iran

"No, Walter. Get on the FDR downtown. I want to get the hell out of this neighborhood."

Once on the FDR, they began to move rapidly south. The traffic was light, but Alex knew that the traffic usually bunched up as they got closer to the downtown area. He said, "Let's go across the Brooklyn Bridge to the Bridge Restaurant. We can call from there."

Patricia called Robert from the pay phone in the lobby of the restaurant, but was told he was at lunch but they would have him get back momentarily. She left the number of the pay phone.

Alex called Elizabeth on his cell phone, but decided not to say anything about the shooting. He did not want to alarm her. He wanted a few moments to figure out what he was going to do. He was certain that the call had puzzled her. He almost never called in the middle of the day.

When he hung up the cell phone began to ring. He answered it, and it was Robert. Alex relayed what had happened. Robert asked to speak to Patricia and Patricia again relayed what had happened.

"I'll be up there in a couple of hours. In the meantime have your driver take you to a taxi stand. Or better yet, have him leave you at the restaurant, and the two of you take a cab to one of the motels near LaGuardia. Spend a minute or two there to make sure you are not followed and then take a cab to the Holiday Inn. Get a room under the name of John Barker. If you can't get a room, I'll look for you in the bar." I'll meet you there as soon as I can get to New York. In the meantime, I'll get some of our people to guard your wife. Where is she?"

"She's at our house in Richmond."

Hanging up the telephone, Alex said, "Let's get a drink and a sandwich."

Patricia answered, "Let's get a quick drink. We can eat when we get to the motel. I'd hate to be caught here because someone spotted the car."

When they reached the Holiday Inn, they were surprised to find Robert waiting for them in the lobby. He said, "I've booked a suite. Why don't we go up there? We can have a drink and talk this over. I know the two of you could use one."

Patricia inquired, "Robert, how did you get here so fast?"

"I happened to be at Andrews Field when I received the call. I was able to get one of the Company jets to take me to LaGuardia."

The suite was on the top floor of the motel with a nice view overlooking LaGuardia Airport. Robert poured drinks for everyone including himself, and they settled into easy chairs and began to talk.

"Tell me what happened," said Robert.

Patricia's clipped reply was, "Robert, we were sitting in a restaurant when two men came in and tried to kill us."

Escape from Iran

Robert Gordon took a sip of his drink. "Yes, I know. But were they after you or someone else?"

Patricia took a sip of her drink. "I really don't know, but I think they were after us."

"Could it have been a case of mistaken identity?"

"Come on, Robert," Patricia answered. "You know better than that"

Alex intervened. "I really think the question is, what do we do from here? Should we cancel our trip? What do we do about the police? Patricia shot one of them in the head, and he's probably dead. The other one may have been hit also. What do we do to protect ourselves, and in my case, my family?"

Robert looked at Alex for a few seconds and answered. "Alex, let me try to answer your questions. First, what do we do! I think you should continue your plans to go to Iran. I think that if the Iranians wanted to kill you, they would want to do it here. They don't want to do it in Iran. It's sort of like the old saying, "The Mafia will never kill you in Las Vegas." They do not want the stigma of your being killed in Iran. Besides, we are not even sure these were Iranians and, whether you want to believe it or not, we are not sure they were trying to kill you and Patricia."

"Come on, Robert. I was there," replied Alex.

"Okay, Alex. Let's take your other questions. About the police. We'll take care of that. In fact, our New York liaison is talking to them now. Neither of you will be involved in any way. Nothing will be in the newspapers. The reports will merely say that the intended victims left the scene and were not able to be identified."

"But Robert, I've been going into that restaurant two or three times a week for better than ten years."

"Do they know your name?"

"No, they don't."

"Well, about all they can find out is that you probably live in the neighborhood. I suppose if the police really wanted to track you down, they could. But I'm telling you that they are not going to want to track you down. So forget it. There's no problem with the shooting. Now let's talk about your family. I think it will be well if Elizabeth could get away somewhere. If I put a guard on your house it could easily expose the fact that you are working with us. My suggestion is that you have her go visit a friend somewhere. However, when you talk to her make sure that you talk over a secure phone.

Your home phone may be tapped. We can talk about that a little more in detail later."

"Now I want to get into the real meat of your mission. We, that is, the U.S. Government, are prepared to grant complete clemency to

Escape from Iran

Robert McClelland and permit him to return here without any fear of prosecution, if he will do us a favor, which we believe is within his power."

Gordon continued, "The Ayatollah Montarezzi is a very conservative and pro western ayatollah. He has a large following in Iran. He is too powerful for the Ayatollah Marzai to kill or imprison, but he is not powerful enough to be able to leave the Iran. In short, he lives because the Ayatollah Marzai is afraid to kill him, but he does not have the freedom to leave the country. He is watched twenty- four hours a day by the radical guards of Marzai."

"Marzai is old and sick. By the law of averages, which I might add Marzai constantly defies, his days are numbered. When he dies there will be a power struggle. There is a good chance that his followers in an attempt to hold their power will then eliminate Monterezzi, who is our main hope for the future.

"He is pro-American. One of the few who are. If we can get him out and keep him on ice until Marzai is out of the picture, we stand a good chance of helping him to take Marzai's place. Obviously we want this. Iran is too strategic for us to permit an antagonistic government. It is a major oil producer and a buffer between Russia and the Middle East. Also, he is one of their top scientists. His knowledge of what is going on will be invaluable to us.

What we want you to do is to persuade McClelland to bring out the Ayatollah Monterezzi. We are told he would very much like to get out of Iran until things change for the better."

Maybe this can be sold, thought Alex. *McClelland really wants to return home.*

"Is this all I have to do?" replied Alex sarcastically, feeling not a bit relieved about his mission to Iran.

"Basically, yes, but we would like for you and Patricia to accompany them when they leave. McClelland trusts you. He might not come out without you to accompany him."

"What about the document granting McClelland immunity? I haven't seen it."

"I have a copy here in my briefcase," replied Gordon, picking up his briefcase from the floor. He opened his briefcase and handed to Alex. "The original signed copy is in my safe at Langley. I'll keep it there until you return home. Obviously you cannot take it or a copy with you to Iran. It would be too dangerous for you to take a copy with you."

"Please have the executed copy delivered by messenger to Ed Wainright, a partner at my Richmond law firm. Have the envelope addressed to me, and marked "Personal and Confidential to be opened by addressee only.""

This is getting worse by the hour, thought Alex. *How did I get into this nightmare?*

"There is one other thing, Alex," continued Gordon. "The Ayatollah has a daughter, whom he will not leave behind."

God help me, thought Alex.

Patricia said nothing. Alex was puzzled. He had the feeling that she liked what she had heard, that this was the sort of adventure which appealed to her.

CHAPTER 28

LATE JANUARY

Three days later Alex and Patricia left for Iran. The executed document granting immunity for Bob McClelland had not been delivered to Alex's law office, as promised by Gordon. This did not bother Alex. He felt it probably took time after Gordon returned to his office to send it by messenger from Washington to Richmond.

Alex's wife Elizabeth had gone to Florida to visit the Atwoods, old friends from Elizabeth's college days. Elizabeth did not know what was going on and was quite angry and apprehensive about Alex's explanation that he suddenly had to go to Europe on business and that she had to go Florida. Although she knew McClelland from the old days, he was afraid to tell her why he was going to Iran to see him.

His friends in Florida, the Atwoods, were equally puzzled when Alex called and practically demanded that they invite Elizabeth for a visit.

Escape from Iran

Gordon promised that Alex's children, who were away at school, would be guarded "day and night'"

Even thought the United States did not maintain diplomatic relations with Iran, the Iranians continued to have an embassy in New York since they were part of the United Nations. Several days later Alex and Patricia went together to the Iranian Embassy. The visas for Iran were issued without incident. It was almost as though there had been no shooting, no attempt on their lives.

Alex had called McClelland by telephone to let him know that they were coming and to give him the flight numbers. McClelland seemed very happy to hear from Alex and said that he would personally meet the plane when it arrived.

They flew on an Air France Concorde to Paris where they transferred to an Air France Flight to Iran. They decided not to stay overnight in Paris for two reasons. First, they did not wish to expose themselves to another possible assassination attempt during an overnight stay in Paris. Second, since the Concorde flight to Paris was only three hours, it made sense to continue on to Tehran, about a two-hour flight from Paris. The flights were again without incident.

When the Tehran flight pulled up to the gate, no one was allowed to disembark from the plane. Two uniformed policemen came aboard and asked for Alex and Patricia by name. Alex's heart sank. He thought, "We're in trouble before we even get off the plane."

G. Gray Garland

Robert Gordon had warned him not to take anything in their baggage or on their person which could get them in trouble with the authorities. Alex was not worried about any problems with customs, but Alex thought that the Iranians were not above framing them.

One of the policemen politely said in English, "Mr. Blair and Miss Diaz, please follow us. Let me help you with your baggage." No other passengers were permitted to leave the plane until Alex and Patricia had disembarked. Alex hoped that the two policemen could not see how nervous he felt. They proceeded off the plane and into the airport.

"Let me have your baggage checks," said the guard who spoke English.

They proceeded through the customs area without stopping and down a corridor to an unmarked door. The guard who had not spoken opened the door and motioned them in.

It was a large wood paneled room furnished with exquisite Persian rugs and overstuffed easy chairs, in three of which were sitting three men who rose as they entered. The man in the center said, "Welcome to Iran."

It was Bob McClelland. He turned to the other two men "I would like to present my two friends from the United States Mr. Alex Blair and his associate, Miss Patricia Diaz."

Escape from Iran

He then turned to Alex and Patricia and said, "I would like to present Mr. Nassar Zarafshan, who is our Deputy Foreign Minister, and Mr. Babak, who is in charge of the Airport here."

Gesturing to easy chairs beside him, McClelland continued, "Your bags will be taken to my car. In the meantime let us have some refreshments. Sit down here beside me Patricia."

By then two white-coated attendants had materialized.

One spoke perfect English." What would you like? Can I offer you coffee or tea? Or if you prefer we can serve you a cocktail? We also have that."

Alex wondered, I *thought alcohol was forbidden in Iran. I could sure use a strong scotch, but I think I should stick to tea.*

Alex was about to reply when Patricia said, "I think I would like a cup of tea, please."

Alex said, "I'd like a cup of tea also, if you please," Alex said.

They made the usual small talk while they had tea and some very delicious cakes that were served with the tea. No one asked them why they had come to Iran or what they did in the United States. It was all very pleasant and polite.

The white-coated attendant appeared again. "The baggage of your guests has been delivered to your car, Mr. McClelland."

"Thank you, Hamid." said McClelland.

Alex thought, *McClelland seems to know everyone, and everyone seems to know McClelland. It's amazing. When we were in school together, I never would have thought McClelland would turn out to be so gregarious. He was rather shy back then. He is really a different person now.*

When they finished their tea and cake, they proceeded out to McClelland's car accompanied by the two Iranian officials and the two policemen who had been waiting outside in the corridor.

Alex was impressed. From his briefings in Virginia, he was certain that McClelland's limousine was parked in the space reserved for the Shah during his days as ruler of Iran. McClelland's car was a big, black Rolls Royce, just like the car he had had in Paris. *Alex thought, It's just like the Queen of England's. In fact,* thought Alex, *It might even be the same car he had in Paris. I doubt it. He probably has two Rolls Royces.*

Behind the Rolls was a black Mercedes sedan. What appeared to be two policemen in khaki uniforms were sitting in the front seat and two other policemen were standing on the sidewalk between the two cars. Both cars bristled with communications antennae.

Iran is not as backwards as I thought, mused Alex as he followed Patricia into the plush back seat of the Rolls.

Driving from the airport, it was difficult to realize that Iran was at war with Iraq. There were no outward signs of the conflict. The streets were busy. Pedestrians and automobiles bustled everywhere. Only to

Escape from Iran

one looking for signs were they detectable. There were fewer cars along the street and most of them showed their age.

Alex wondered, *Despite all of this, McClelland has a new Rolls Royce and cars for his bodyguards. It was pretty obvious he does know the right people.*

They proceeded up a high hill and turned off the main road onto a tree-lined driveway which wound for some distance through well-manicured lawns and gardens until they arrived at a very large building. McClelland waived his hand in the direction of the building and exclaimed, "Welcome to my home."

McClelland's house was truly a palace. It was situated upon what appeared to be considerable acreage with wooded areas and extensive gardens. As the car pulled to a stop in front of the house, several servants appeared to unload the guests luggage. Alex and Patricia were awestruck as they entered the house.

It was truly a massive palace, an architectural masterpiece, but everything was in excellent taste. The house contained many large rooms with magnificent furnishings. It was truly impressive. Neither Alex nor Patricia had ever seen anything to equal it. They were absolutely awed by it.

McClelland explained that his home had belonged to the Shah's sister, Princess Ashcraff, and that after the coup he had purchased it from the present government together with its furnishings. Pointing

G. Gray Garland

out many of the paintings and much of the furniture, he told Alex and Patricia about its history.

Truly, any museum would have been happy to have such a collection of paintings and furniture. In fact, McClelland's house had been a small palace. It was originally built by the Shah as a guesthouse for visiting dignitaries. However, his sister liked it so much that she persuaded the Shah to give it to her to be used as her principal residence in Tehran, and she had used it as her residence for many years.

CHAPTER 29

FEBRUARY 1984

The next morning before breakfast, Alex had an opportunity to wander through McClelland's palace. The main living room was furnished with antique French furniture, each piece of museum quality. On the walls hung a collection of paintings that any major art museum, including the Metropolitan in New York, would have envied. Van Dyke, El Greco, Renoir, Manet, and Monet to name a few. Alex examined some of the paintings closely. To the best of his knowledge the ones he examined appeared to be originals.

McClelland's den, which was huge by American standards, but small by the size of the other rooms, was tastefully furnished, and, surprisingly, with early American antique furniture. Alex and Elizabeth collected early American antiques, and he easily determined that these were the best pieces he had ever seen, including some at the Metropolitan Museum in New York.

G. Gray Garland

A lovely Rhode Island block front chest stood here, and a magnificent Philadelphia highboy there. Alex mused there must be at least ten million dollars worth of furniture in this room alone. On walls of the den were hung paintings by American artists. Alex recognized paintings by Winslow Homer, Bierstadt, and Childe Hassam. There was even a magnificent harbor scene by the well-known contemporary marine artist John Stobart.

Alex suddenly felt very uneasy. He began to wonder. *Is McClelland going to give up all of this to return to the United States? He'll never get this out of the Iran. Never. I don't know. I wonder if we are getting into a trap.*

About that time, McClelland strolled into the room. "How do you like my house, Alex?"

"It's magnificent, Bob. Utterly magnificent. I've never seen such a collection of American paintings and antiques in my life. Where did you get them?"

"Oh, I've been collecting them for more than fifteen years. I get all of the catalogs from Christie's and Sotheby's and other places, and I have my agents bid on the pieces I think I would like. In the beginning, if a piece was shipped to me and I didn't like it, they would permit me to return it and waive their fee since I was such a large customer. However, for the past few years if I didn't like it, I merely stored it. Now I've got a warehouse full of paintings and furniture. Once in awhile I

Escape from Iran

give something away, but mostly it just gathers dust. Now let's have breakfast. We are going to eat on the terrace."

Alex thought, *Isn't it a little cool for that*, but said nothing, and followed McClelland. They went through several rooms and arrived at a lovely room with glass on three sides.

"So this is the terrace?"

"Yes, it's very pleasant. You feel like you are outside. You have a great view of the city, and you are comfortable on a cool day. I usually have breakfast here."

A small table was set for two, and two servants in white coats stood by.

Again, Alex thought, *Is Bob really going to leave all of this? We had better be very careful.*

As they sat down, McClelland said, "I understand Patricia wants to sleep in this morning, so I thought we'd go ahead without her."

One of the servants took their orders, the other poured coffee and retired a discreet distance away.

"Speaking of antiques, look at this one," McClelland said, pulling a photograph from his pocket. "I hear you are a collector of early American furniture." The photograph was of a Rhode Island block front chest.

"The price is on the back", said McClelland.

Alex turned the photograph over and was surprised to read the words.

"Do not talk business unless I initiate the conversation." Under that was "$235,000 U.S."

Alex returned the photograph. "It's too rich for my blood. It's nice to know someone who can afford such expensive furniture."

McClelland dismissed this remark with a shrug and said, "Alex, I want to show you the view from the far end of this terrace."

As McClelland pointed to several points of interest in the valley below, he said, "Alex, what did you find out about my being able to return to the states?"

Alex, trying not to look around to see if the bodyguards were nearby, replied, "Bob, the United States is willing to grant you immunity if you will persuade the Ayatollah Montazeri to come out of the Iran with you. They believe that because of his pro-Western feelings he would likely be willing to flee from Iran."

McClelland did not say anything for a few moments. Then he said, "I know the ayatollah very well. I have worked with him for many years. He is not only an ayatollah, he is also a scientist. He has worked with me on many occasions in purchasing goods and services from the West. However, there may be a problem. His wife died many years ago. He has one child, a daughter, whom he worships. He would never leave Iran without taking her with him."

Alex quickly replied, "Then, we'll make arrangements to take her with us too."

CHAPTER 30

On the day after their arrival in Iran McClelland suggested that Alex and Patricia might like to go sightseeing and shopping, Alex replied that they would very much like to go sightseeing and shopping, if McClelland was sure he could spare the time. Alex said he would like to purchase a piece of jewelry for his wife. He did not tell McClelland the name of the shop he had been told to go to by the CIA, but fortunately this was one of the shops that McClelland suggested.

They went into the shop, and Alex was surprised. The shop looked more like it belonged in the high-rent district of New York rather than in Iran. Alex ordered a ruby ring for Elizabeth and requested that it be engraved with her initials and an inscription, "To Elizabeth with all my love forever" together with the date. The owner said that the ring would be ready later in the afternoon.

Looking Alex straight in his eyes, the owner said, "Here is a very nice wristwatch. I'm sure it is something you would like" Alex examined the watch and reading the signal in the shop owner's eyes said, "I do like that watch. I'll take it also."

"You can pick it up when you pick up the ring."

Alex replied, "I might as well take it now."

Winking at Alex the shop owner said, "You can pay for it when you pick up the ring. Any friend of Mr. McClelland is automatically a friend of mine."

Alex was not puzzled by the watch. It appeared to be an ordinary watch, but he recognized it from his visit to Virginia. .

That afternoon Alex and McClelland returned to the shop to pick up the ruby ring he had ordered for his wife. He was still amazed that such a shop could exist, considering the economic conditions in Iran. They went in. There was only one clerk, not the owner, who had been there before, but another man was also present, dressed in a morning coat.

"Ah, Mr. McClelland, Mr. Blair, so nice to see you. I presume you have come for the ring you ordered."

He then picked up a black leather jewelry case, opened it, and showed them the lovely diamond and ruby ring. "

The owner came in and greeted them. He picked up the ring. "It's quite lovely isn't it? It used to belong to the Shah. You know, in the old days I used to sell a lot of the Shah's jewelry. So much jewelry was given to him by people seeking favors and by visiting dignitaries from abroad

Escape from Iran

that he disposed of much of it. Of course, he kept the very fine objects, but I used to sell much of his excess jewelry. Some I sold here in the shop, but mostly I sold it through jewelers throughout the world. In any event, I know your wife will like the ring."

As Alex stooped over to examine it, the manager, again looking him in the eye, said, "Here is your receipt. Please make sure it is correct. You will need it for your Customs people when you return. I know. I used to sell a lot of jewelry to Americans."

Alex looked at the receipt. There was a note, which said. "Your instructions are in the lining."

"Here, let me wrap it for you. You had better keep the receipt. You will need it when you go through customs in the United States."

Alex took the receipt. He was not surprised to see the the receipt with the note on it was now a real receipt. "Thank you very much. I'm sure my wife will like it."

With that they left the shop and returned to McClelland's home.

Alex opened the jewelry case in the quiet of his room and carefully pulled back the lining and removed several neatly folded sheets of paper

He read them carefully. When they picked up the ayatollah and his daughter, they were to proceed to a safe house which had been arranged. This safe house was not a house at all but rather several rooms in a downtown office building. They were to proceed to the rear of the office building where they would be met and taken to their quarters on the top floor by a freight elevator. There they would wait until the agency determined that it was safe to attempt to leave Tehran. They would receive additional instructions when they reached the safe house. Clothes and other props would be in the car. They should put on these to change their appearance as much as possible to look like Iranians in the unlikely event that someone saw them entering the office building. Alex was to remember the instructions and immediately destroy the message.

There was also the wristwatch radio, which Alex had been instructed how to operate in Virginia. He decided to test it at the first opportunity.

As soon as he was alone, Alex decided to test his radio. When he pressed the button to send his message the LCD screen showed the words "Call Burt at 8224."

Alex knew that the message meant that he should look for a name on page 8 of the paperback he was reading about Iran. That would give him a message, which he would decipher by adding and subtracting digits to the numbers given to him on the screen. The message when he decoded it merely acknowledged the receipt of his transmission. There were no instructions.

McClelland had already suggested that Alex should not use the telephone in his house to say anything confidential from his house. He

Escape from Iran

was worried about the lines being tapped. Alex was very happy to have the radio. At least he had some link with home.

When Alex and Bob went onto the terrace Patricia joined them for lunch. They had lunch on the same dining terrace that Alex and McClelland had used for their breakfast. The sun had come out and it was now a beautiful day.

It appeared to Alex that Bob was being very careful to allay any suspicion. It was very possible that one or more of the servants was a spy for the Government, and he felt it was better to be careful than sorry.

When they had finished their lunch, McClelland gestured at the scenery and said, "It's a lovely day. Would you like to go horseback riding? The trails are nice, and you might enjoy the scenery."

Both Patricia and Alex said, "Yes, but Patricia noted that they did not have any riding clothes."

"No problem, we have everything." It was truly a lovely, sunny day. Alex and Patricia were led by McClelland to a large closet filled with riding apparel, boots, riding pants, and other accessories, They were soon dressed for riding. When they met McClelland, he remarked, "Patricia, you look like you came out of a fashion magazine."

"Thanks Bob. It was all your riding clothes."

The air was crisp and clear. McClelland led them along the riding trail. They were always followed, somewhat discreetly, by two bodyguards who were also on horseback.

Alex wondered if the bodyguards could monitor their conversations. He had read of some incredible eavesdropping devices. *Probably not here*, hr thought In any event, there had not been any conversations to monitor.

McClelland reined up at the top of a hill. Alex and Patricia rode up beside him. "I thought you would enjoy the view from here," he said, sweeping his arm in the direction of the valley below. "You will meet the Ayatollah Montazeri in two days. I want our observers to relax a little before we do anything drastic. I suspect that some of my people are spies for Marzai, so we must be careful. I do not want to appear to be in intense conversations with you. Be patient! It will all work out."

With that he rode away. It took a few seconds for Alex and Patricia to recover from his remarks and to follow him down the trail.

Afterwards most of the balance of the day was spent driving around sightseeing, always in the company of McClelland's bodyguards. No mention was made of their mission.

CHAPTER 31

After several more days of nothing happening, Alex was becoming very nervous about the arrangements or rather the lack of them. He did not want to proceed without meeting the Ayatollah Montarzeri and agreeing upon a coordinated plan of action. Also nothing had transpired regarding the Iranians purchasing metals from him. No meetings had been arranged. Alex wondered if perhaps the Iranians did not want to push the matter, but wanted Alex to try and relax and enjoy himself for a few days before bringing up possible business transactions.

McClelland said that the Ayatollah Montazeri continued to insist that he was afraid to meet Alex for fear that he might be seen. If this happened, the game would be over for all of them.

Alex finally agreed that he would be satisfied if he could see the ayatollah, and his daughter, even if it were from a distance, and if the ayatollah gave him some prearranged signal.

It was finally decided to ask the Ayatollah to be in front of the main Mosque at eleven o'clock two days hence, and that as McClelland's car drove by he would hand a large book to his daughter and check his left shoe as though he had something in

In the meantime Alex continued to worry. He had heard nothing about the PC&R deal. He could lose it by being away. He had yet to be contacted by anyone from the CIA. His escape equipment had not been delivered, and he still had not met with any Iranian officials concerning the reason for his visit. When he queried McClelland about a meeting with the Iranian officials interested in purchasing so-called "exotic" metals, Bob always said, "Be patient. We don't operate on a fast track like you do in the States."

The equipment for their escape from Iran had not been delivered, but as he was walking down a hallway one of the servants hummed the prearranged password, and gave to Alex a note, which when he later read it stated that the equipment was ready, and that it would be delivered to the safe house when they arrived there. If, in an emergency, and only if in a grave emergency, Alex wanted to meet the CIA agent, he could do so on Monday, Wednesday and Friday at 10:00 a.m. or 8:00 p.m. by going to the taxi stand at the Hotel Metropole and finding a green Mercedes taxicab with a bent right rear fender and with the number 13 on its door.

Alex was not terribly superstitious, but the number "13" did not raise his flagging spirits.

CHAPTER 32

The next day at breakfast McClelland announced that he had some business to take care of and that he would be gone most of the day.

After breakfast Alex walked with him to his waiting car. Most of the conversation was small talk. McClelland obviously figured there were listening devices planted throughout his house. However, as they walked from the house to the car McClelland quietly informed him that he was going to meet the Ayatollah Montazeri so that they could arrange the time and place for Alex to meet with him and plan the ayatollah's escape from Iran.

When McClelland returned that evening, he informed Alex and Patricia that the ayatollah was still afraid of meeting Alex. He feared the possibility of their being seen together, but he and his daughter would be standing in front of the main mosque at an agreed time. Even though Alex had said this would be okay, it still upset Alex.

"My instructions were that I should meet the ayatollah and make certain that he really wants to defect. In fact, I was instructed to make certain that the person I contact is in fact the Ayatollah Montazeri. I have been given information, which I can use to verify he is who he says he is."

McClelland did not argue. "I'll see what I can do. However, I think it is very risky for both of you."

The next day McClelland met again with the ayatollah and made the new suggestion. When McClelland returned he told Alex, "The ayatollah is still afraid to meet with you. You don't know how suspicious these people are. If for one moment they had an inkling of what you planned, all of us would be in trouble, big, big, trouble! These people play rough. There would be no trial; just slow death by some horrible torture."

McClelland continued, "However all is not lost. Tomorrow you and Patricia will go shopping at one of our Bazaars for trinkets and souvenirs. The ayatollah will also be at central bazaar with his daughter. You will pass each other at one of the counters. You will be too far away for you to exchange messages, but you will be close enough to clearly identify the ayatollah to make certain that you know he has received your message and wants to escape Iran with you. The ayatollah will be carrying two books under his left arm. As you become aware of each other, he will shift the books to his right arm.

CHAPTER 33

Five days had passed since Alex and Patricia had "eyeballed" the ayatollah and his daughter at the Mosque. Although Alex was very uneasy with this arrangement, he was now convinced that the Ayatollah really did desire to escape with them.

In the meantime to convince the Iranians that Alex's visit was for business purposes as well as to renew his acquaintance with him, McClelland told Alex he had told the Iranians to arrange for Alex to meet with the Iranians who were in charge of purchasing metals. However, nothing definite had been decided by the Iranians with respect to what they wished to buy. Alex was becoming increasingly apprehensive. He wondered whether the few Iranians he had met were merely testing him to make sure he was genuine and would be really willing to sell to them knowing it was against the laws of the United States.

When McClelland returned early the next afternoon, he told Alex and Patricia that the Iranian Director of Purchasing had requested a meeting with Alex for tomorrow morning, at which they would discuss

G. Gray Garland

the possibility of buying certain metals from Alex's company. "As you know, one of the reasons I was able to invite you here is that I told the Iranians that you owned Mercer Metals and perhaps could be persuaded to sell to us some of the metals that we really need. They have pressed me about this, but what I told them was that I wanted you to have a relaxing time sightseeing before I approached you about having the meeting. I was supposed to soften you up and persuade you that you could sell to us without any great personal risk to yourself. Now they want to meet with us to verify that you would be willing or not willing to sell metals to us." McClelland continued saying that he did not know all of the engineers who would be at the meeting, but he did know the director of purchasing, whom he was certain would be there. They were standing on the terrace to divert the attention of anyone watching them, McClelland pointed at a landmark in the distance and continued, "In any event you should be prepared to answer any questions that they may throw at you." McClelland pointed to another landmark and said, "I know that the metals that they particularly need are the metals which are primarily used in missiles. I suggest that you tell them you're not sure you can do this because it is illegal. They may then ask you what is the price that you sell this metal for in the United States. You should tell them the truth-what the real price is. They will likely already know what you're selling it for, so do not be cute and give them the wrong price. You can also stall giving them a final answer by

Escape from Iran

saying you have to go back to the United States and check your melting schedules to determine what metals will be available. You cannot just take these metals from an existing contract without bringing it to the attention of the government and you are not about to try to find out on the telephone for obvious reasons,"

The next morning McClelland and Alex drove to a government building in downtown Tehran. Alex was surprised they did not go in McClelland's opulent Rolls-Royce, but in a five- or six-year-old tan Mercedes sedan. Alex recognized the driver as the same one who usually drove the Rolls-Royce. There was a car following them with McClelland's ever present bodyguards.

The building, in which they were to meet, was a rather drab five-story office building. The obvious difference from other nearby office buildings was that this building was surrounded by a fence topped with barbed wire. Also there were uniformed guards at the gate to the fence and at the entrance to the building. Both sets of guards asked for identification, but upon giving their names, Alex and McClelland entered the building without any problems. They were directed to an office on the third floor. After riding a rickety, old elevator they were then led to a smoked-filled conference room. It seemed that almost everyone in Iran smoked. Alex even noticed two packs of Marlboros on the table. They obviously preferred American cigarettes. The room was bare of any decorations, except for a large framed photo of the

Ayatollah Marzai. The walls were a dirty white, and the windows had not been washed for a very long time.

There were eight Iranians sitting around the large conference table. This was no surprise. Alex had done business in other countries where there were always a large number of the countrymen in meetings. Six were dressed in the flowing robes that Arabs in Iran normally wore. One wore a military uniform. The other was dressed in a Western styled suit. He seemed to be a leader of some sort. He was dressed in a well tailored, expensive looking dark suit with a white shirt and what appeared to be a striped, regimental or club tie. For several minutes there were the usual introductions back and forth with much handshaking and with each of the Iranians in Arab robes giving Alex their business card. Although they had been introduced by name, no card was given Alex by the man in the military uniform or the man in the stylish suit. *Odd,* thought Alex.

Tea was then served. The usual small talk followed. "Did you have a nice trip?" one of the men asked. "How do you like Iran?" asked another. All spoke English, some better than others.

The Iranian in the dark suit spoke in perfect English, "I hope you had no trouble arranging your trip." The way he said it gave Alex a chilling feeling of unease as he remembered the shooting in New York. He could not understand the feeling of hostility he felt.

Escape from Iran

Finally they got down to business. The Iranian sitting at the head of the table, who appeared to be the senior member of the purchasing group, also speaking fluent English, asked Alex about Mercer Metals and what metals it produced. Alex took quite a bit of time to explain about his company and its products. As the talks continued, an interpreter reported what was said for those who apparently did not speak English or understand enough to follow the conversations,.

Then the conversations took a strange turn. The Iranian in the Saville Row dark suit sitting across the table from Alex took over the questioning. He spoke fluent English. Instead of asking Alex about Mercer Metals, he asked Alex a number of personal questions, which, to Alex, seemed completely irrelevant in connection with the possible sale of metals to the Iranians. He finally said to Alex, "Mr. Blair, you know, of course, the United States has sanctions preventing you from selling any metals to us."

Alex, who had been schooled in advance how to answer a question such as this replied, "I am not really familiar with any sanctions. To the best of my knowledge we have never encountered this. We have never had any problems with respect to whom we sold our metals."

"Do you sell any metals into France?"

"Yes, we have several customers in France."

"Then I would presume that you would be willing to sell your metals to a French company?"

169

G. Gray Garland

"Yes, I don't know why not, but I would not want to do anything that is against the laws of my country."

Snuffing out his third or fourth cigarette (Alex had lost count) the man in the dark suit said, "Let's just say that you would have no reason to believe you were selling product to a French company that may or may not in turn be selling this metal to us."

Again, relying on his schooling at the CIA in Virginia Alex replied, "I would have to think very carefully on that. I do not want to get in trouble with my own country."

The Iranian did not let up. "Suppose we made this very worthwhile to you personally. We could pay your company a premium price, and we could pay you a very, very handsome commission deposited in your account at a Swiss bank."

Alex picked up his teacup, hoping his hands would not shake and show how nervous he was. He paused for a moment as if thinking about how to respond, as the CIA had trained him to do. He took a sip of tea, and then answered, "Let me think about that. Either Mr. McClelland or I will get back to you before I leave Iran."

The senior Iranian replied, "Give it some thought, Mr. Blair. We would not want to do anything to harm you."

Harm me" thought Alex. *My God, what am I into? Will I get out of this alive?*

Escape from Iran

Alex's answer seemed to satisfy the Iranians, for within several minutes the meeting was over. There were more handshakes. Alex left relieved to get out of the meeting, but also he felt very uncomfortable and uneasy about the meeting.

On the ride home both Alex and McClelland were careful not to talk about their true thoughts on the meeting. But as prearranged, Alex did say for the benefit of the driver who was probably listening to every word, "I do think I shall do it. However, I've got to be very sure I don't get caught." Both Alex and McClelland were certain Alex's remarks would be reported.

Once they were alone, Alex and McClelland discussed the meeting and their true thoughts. Bob told Alex then he did not know the Iranian who was proposing the deal to Alex. He knew some of the other Iranians in the meeting, but several of them were completely new to him. He suspected they might be intelligence agents. In any event they both felt the meeting had gone as well as they could have expected..

CHAPTER 34

The next afternoon when he and McClelland were riding horseback. As they topped a hill, McClelland reined in his horse and pointing to a distant landmark said, "We're going to go tonight."

On hearing this Alex shuddered and blurted, "We really are?" He quickly recovered and thought, *How did Bob hear this? I'm the one who should be contacted? Is he a CIA Agent? I do not understand this. I'm sure I will find out sooner or later.* When he started to question McClelland, McClelland did not answer him and rode away This left Alex more perplexed than ever.

If this was the night, it was a good choice. It had turned dark, cold and rainy. *A perfect night for subversive activity or much better, thought Alex, to be home in bed in the good old USA with an interesting book,*

Using McClelland's jet to escape was out of the question. They had never even considered this. The pilots were Iranian Air Force officers, and none of them, including Patricia, who had a pilot's license, felt they could handle the big jet.

Escape from Iran

After pouring over maps of the city and much heated discussion Alex, McClelland and Patricia had finally agreed on an escape plan. It was relatively simple, and it should work. It only involved only the three of them, so there should be little chance of leaks or slipups.

McClelland said he could arrange for the disguises and the vehicles to use. "There is an old taxi that has been parked near my warehouse for sometime. There apparently was not enough business for the old vehicle, so the owner just parked it there. I'll arrange to get it and make sure it will run."

Alex replied, trying not to look nervous, "How are we going to get out of here with all of your bodyguards watching our every move?"

"We'll pretend to go to bed early. When they see we're going to bed, the bodyguards usually leave to go home, and thereafter the kitchen help and most of the other servants also go home. A few have cars, but they mostly have to take taxis. The taxis are allowed to come onto the grounds and pick them up. I will arrange for a taxi to come later after the bodyguards have gone home. I don't think the guards at the gate will even look at the taxi, because it's so usual to see some of the help going home in taxis later in the evening.

"The Ayatollah and his daughter regularly dine with a friend, and after dinner they then walked or took a cab to their nearby home. On the night of escape the taxi would be driven by me, in disguise.

I would even have a fake beard, which would be given to each of us, including Patricia. I would pick up the Ayatollah and his daughter and drive them to the rendezvous. I would follow an agreed route, passing Alex, who would be parked on a side street. If it appeared he was being followed Alex would radio Patricia, who was parked near the entrance to a narrow side street several blocks away in a large truck, which I have already procured.. She would let me go by and then block the street with the truck. She would then run through an alleyway to the next street where Alex, going around the block, would pick her up, and then they would proceed to the first rendezvous point, which is near an old warehouse. There, they would abandon the escape vehicles inside the warehouse and leave by a panel truck parked there before going to the second hideaway, which is not too far away. I would meet them there and take the truck to a market area several blocks away where I would leave it. If all went well, it should be several days or more before the parked truck would be noticed."

It had been decided that they would not try to leave Tehran on the first night. If the ayatollah's escape was noticed, the city and the highways out of the city would be swarming with police and soldiers. There would be roadblocks everywhere. It would be almost impossible to escape from Tehran. All vehicles leaving would be stopped and searched.

Escape from Iran

They would have to hunker down for a few days or maybe even a week. For Alex this was a very depressing thought. He was needed at home. His big deal might go down the drain if he didn't show up, but most of all, he wanted to get out of Iran alive.

The CIA had chosen an office building as the hideaway. It was an older building in which many of the offices were vacant. Inasmuch as business conditions were very poor, several entire floors were vacant. They had stocked an office suite with food and bedding- enough, if necessary, to allow them to stay there for months without being found.

CHAPTER 35

When they arrived at the back alley door to the office building, their safe house, they were met by a rather bedraggled looking man in Iranian dress, who surprised them by introducing himself in excellent English.

"My name is Felix. Follow me I will take you up to your quarters." Alex was greatly relieved that "Felix" had finally contacted them. He had been briefed before his trip that an agent using the name "Felix" would likely contact them.

Without any further conversation they followed him into the building and into a nearby freight elevator. Felix proceeded to remove a wooden wedge from the elevator door. He had obviously used this to keep anyone else from using the elevator.

"When we get to our floor be quiet, and don't get off until I give you the signal that all is clear. If it is not clear I will raise my left hand slightly, like this, and we will proceed up another floor and wait until

Escape from Iran

the coast is clear. The floor above our floor is vacant so there should be no one there."

When the elevator reached the eighth floor, which was their destination, Felix peered out and gave the all-clear signal. They proceeded a few feet down the hall to what appeared to be a janitor's closet. Felix opened the door, and after fumbling around for a moment inside a closet filled with buckets, mops, and cleaning materials, opened a small door on the left wall of the closet.

Felix motioned them through the door and then quickly followed, closing the door behind them. Once the closet doors were closed he switched on the lights. They appeared to be in a small supply room. There were shelves and supply bins on each of the walls. Felix then opened another door. This one led into what appeared to be a suite of offices.

He then said, "Let me show you your new home".

The "safe house" was very comfortable. It consisted of a suite of seven rooms obviously designed for use as an executive suite of offices. Each private office contained a couch upon which one could sleep comfortably. There was a men's room and a ladies' room, and off of one of the large private offices there was a complete bathroom with a shower. There was even a kitchenette that contained a refrigerator and a stove.

G. Gray Garland

Felix more or less herded them into a fairly large conference room. Once they were there, he announced that the CIA had sent him to meet them. He further stated that the offices had been rented several years ago as a safe house at the time of the hostage crisis during the Presidency of Jimmy Carter. The agency felt that it was probably the last place that searchers would look would be an office building, especially one where so much of the space was occupied by tenants. Iranian workers came to work at a Iranian company which occupied part of the space, but the safe house portion was segregated from that section, so that even these people would not likely know that the so called unoccupied portion of the office could be used, in fact, to shelter fugitives. All in all it was a very clever set up. If for some reason the authorities inspected the offices, there were desks and all the normal things you would find in an office. If they asked why this portion was unoccupied, it was very easy to say that it had been set up during the time of the Shah when things were prosperous, and that the space had not been able to be rented, but had been retained hoping for better times.

The only news they got from the outside at the safe house was through Felix. There was a television set, but apparently there was no news being broadcast about the ayatollah's disappearance. However, Felix told them when he next visited that there was quite a furor over his disappearance and also that of McClelland. There were roadblocks everywhere. The airports had been closed and the borders sealed. The

Escape from Iran

government was taking no chances of their getting out of Iran. All of McClelland's household servants and many of his office staff had been arrested, even those on the government payroll. Apparently they trusted no one. No reason had been given publicly for all of this, but rumors on the street were that it had something to do with Iraqi commandos who had parachuted into the country.

So the group hunkered down and waited. For the first day or so everyone was tense, almost expecting to see the door suddenly battered down and swarms of Iranian police, guns drawn, come pouring through the doorway.

At least we are on the move and probably safe for the moment thought Alex sipping a scotch, which Felix had produced.

CHAPTER 36

In Washington, D.C. it was about 8:45 in the morning. Word that Blair and McClelland had disappeared and that Iran was in turmoil and looking for them had reached Langley. The director, when he had received word at home about midnight had called for an emergency meeting for the next morning at in his conference room. He had briefed the president at 7:00 a.m. The President seemed pleased, but he was non committal. This puzzled Cabot. He was both elated and apprehensive. On the one hand the plan seemed to be working. The president seemed pleased. On the other hand they still had to get Blair, McClelland et al out of Iran. Robert Gordon had great confidence in Felix, but they were not out of Iran yet.

Rose Mitchell, the director's secretary was also present at the meeting, sometimes taking notes and sometimes filling coffee cups from the percolator on the sideboard.

The Operation Fishhook group had been told to assemble in the director's conference room. He was not there. They waited somewhat

Escape from Iran

anxiously fidgeting for about ten minutes. As soon as he entered from his private office, they all felt something good must have happened. He was not a good poker player, and he was even worse at hiding good news. He appeared jaunty, almost dancing into the room with a smirk or smile on his face.

Before sitting down he announced, "I received good news last night. Blair and McClelland and the Ayatollah are on the run and are hiding in a safe house."

Robert Gordon already knew this since Felix worked directly for him, but he said nothing.

The director took a cup of coffee from Rose with a nod and continued, "When I met with the President this morning, he was enthusiastic about what we're doing."

Mike Hogan the Director of Covert Actions, who also knew about what was happening, thought, *He looks like a movie star with his hair perfectly groomed, wearing one of his beautiful well-cut suits. And really he must know that most of us had been notified about midnight that a satellite signal had been received from Felix announcing that McClelland, the Ayatollah, and Blair had gone into hiding at the safe house and that Iran was in turmoil looking for them.*

The assistant director with some slight sarcasm asked, "That's fine, but how are you going to get them out of Iran?"

G. Gray Garland

The director, somewhat flippantly, answered, "Through Turkey, of course. We are going to keep them in a safe house long enough for the Iranians to settle down. Then they can go out through Turkey. They cannot keep their borders close and their airports watched forever."

"How long do you think that will take?" It was the assistant director.

"As long as necessary."

"It might be quite a long time."

"Well, we'll have to wait as long as is necessary."

The Director continued. "Just make sure they don't try to go out through Iraq or Russia. I am very pleased at how things are going. Keep me informed on this."

He stood up and went into his private office closing the door behind him without another word to the assembled group.

CHAPTER 37

They had been in the "safe house" hideaway for some five days. They were sitting in the conference room of the office suite when Felix, the CIA agent, announced, "Tomorrow we leave."

He continued "You have all been given proper clothing so you that will blend in with the Iranians. I want a dress inspection tonight to make sure that all of you are dressed so that you will indeed look like the natives. Alex, you and Bob and Patricia don't have to put on your beards until tomorrow morning, but I do want to check your clothes tonight.

"Tomorrow there will be two cars parked around the corner. One will be a dirty, grey 1980 Chevrolet sedan and the other will be a dirty, white 1981 Toyota station wagon. Don't let their beat up appearance fool you. They are both in excellent condition. They both have their gas tanks full and several cans of gasoline, so you should have more than enough gas to get you to the border. Also there will be extra cans at each stop.

"We will leave the building one or two at a time and walk to the cars. In this way no one will by chance see us all together and report a suspicious group leaving from the back of this building. Also, I can station myself across the street from the cars, and if it appears you are being followed, I can warn both you and the drivers of the cars. Obviously I cannot contact you if you are being followed, so what I'll do is warn you. My signal that you are being followed will be that I'll be leaning against a car reading a newspaper.

"If you see that signal, do not panic. Take time to shake your followers. I will show you on a map several ways that I think you can shake them. After you believe you are no longer being followed return to the car. Again, if I signal you that you are being followed, you will have to make another attempt to shake your followers. If for some reason you cannot shake your followers, we will have someone watch for you in front of this address. There will be someone there every morning at seven-thirty watching for you to go by. His signal will be to carry a rolled newspaper in his left hand like this. Our lookout will look for you, but don't expect to see him. We do not wish to expose any of our people in the event you are followed. If you are not followed, you will be contacted and led to a car. You will be able to identify your contact he will approach you and ask you in English if you would like to purchase a cheap Swiss self-winding wristwatch."

Escape from Iran

Felix then placed a large map of Iran on the conference table and continued "The Iranians are not certain whether or not you have escaped, but since you have not appeared in the West, they will not be taking any chances. They will continue the increased guards and patrols along the borders and at all crossing points. They will expect you to try to get across the border into Turkey. It's the closest friendly border," he continued pointing at the map. "And they know that the United States is very influential there. In fact, we have several military installations there, including a large air force base, from which you could be flown to the States.

"Iraq is out of the question. As you know, they are not friendly with the United States. Afghanistan is also pretty much out of the question. With the war on there, it would be too difficult for you to get through safely to Pakistan. Pakistan would be okay. It's friendly with the U.S., but it's just too far away, and you would have to travel too many miles across Iran to get there. The chances of your being spotted by the Iranians would be greatly increased.

"Russia is not friendly with the U.S., so they would not expect you to go there. Therefore I am certain that they will concentrate most of their efforts along the Turkish border.

"So what are we going to do?" Patricia said speaking for the first time.

G. Gray Garland

"We are going to surprise them. "We are going to get out of here through Russia."

"How is that possible?" exclaimed Alex.

"That's not possible," simultaneously gasped a very nervous McClelland.

"Oh, but it is", said Felix. "The Russians don't like Marzai any more than we do. Therefore they are more than willing to help us get the ayatollah out of Iran, providing no one can tie them into helping us. It's all been arranged.

"Now let me go over the map with you. From Tehran you will go south toward Qom. That's where the Ayatollah Marzai lives. They will never expect you to leave the city in that direction. About thirty miles south there is a dirt road that goes to Veramin. At Veramin you will find a good highway that goes to Semnan and on to the Russian border.

"I doubt that they will be watching this route. You should not have any trouble until you reach the Russian border, and I think we have this problem solved. You will continue East to Darreh Gaz, near the border. There you will take a trail through the mountains into Russia."

No one slept very well that night. Alex gave up trying to sleep about four o'clock and wandered down the hall to the kitchenette where to his surprise he found Felix, McClelland and the Ayatollah sitting around the kitchen table drinking tea.

Escape from Iran

"You'll never get any sleep, if you sit up all night drinking tea", he said to no one in particular.

No one answered him.

After what seemed like a long pause. Felix said, "Alex may I get you a cup of tea."

Alex, rubbing his eyes, answered, "Oh sure, I don't plan to go back to sleep. Anything new?"

"No, not as far as I know. We're all set. I'll check to make sure the cars are all in place and give all of you a last-minute briefing before we move out. I don't anticipate any trouble. Everything should go as we planned it."

Throughout the wee hours of the morning the others drifted into the kitchenette. What conversation there was, was sporadic and disjointed. Someone would say, "I'll be glad when we get back to the States."

After a long pause someone else would mutter, "So will I," or there would be no answer.

At about six thirty Felix said, "I would like everyone to gather in the large office, so I can give you some final instructions."

When they were all present and settled Felix again went over the plans of how they would leave the building in small groups and proceed down the back alleyway to the street and then to the waiting automobiles. Part of the group was to turn left at the end of alleyway

G. Gray Garland

and proceed a block and a half to where their car would be waiting. The other group was to turn right and proceed two blocks to where their car would be waiting.

Then came the surprises.

"When you leave this building my job ends. You are going to have to get to your destination on your own. These are my orders. I can't do anything about them. I have given McClelland a map and the necessary information to get you to your destination. I have also given a map and information to Reza, the ayatollah's daughter. She and Patricia and the ayatollah will go in the second car. Alex and Bob will go in the first car. Each car will have someone who can speak Farsi and a walkie-talkie, so that if there is trouble, you can warn each other.

"Alex, your walkie-talkie is in this loaf of bread. You open the loaf and there it is. Patricia, your walkie-talkie is in this jar when you press under the spout and twist, the top comes off and there it is. I don't need to explain their operation again, but I do want to warn you that you should not rely on them for a distance beyond five miles. The second car should follow at least a half-mile or so behind the first car. Obviously you will keep your walkie-talkies out so that you can talk, but be prepared to hide them quickly should you run into a roadblock. Again, obviously, our plan is not without some danger. I would prefer to have send firepower with you, but I can't spare any people. They will likely be looking for a party of five. I don't believe that two women

Escape from Iran

dressed as men and a man will seem suspicious. That is why I am having Patricia and the ayatollah and his daughter go in the second car. Also, Bob and Alex, I don't think they will be looking for two men. Therefore your chances should be very good. Patricia is a professional that's why I want her to go with the ayatollah."

"And we're expendable. That's why you want us to go first", muttered Alex, buttoning his shirt.

"No, not at all, if you want to change the order, it's okay with me. Bob knows the country and he speaks Farsi. It seems to me that gives you a pretty good chance."

The next surprise followed. "Bob, I would like you and Alex and Patricia to come with me a minute."

They followed Felix down the hall to what was obviously a supply room. Felix pulled back a curtain and there on the table was a collection of firearms, Uzis, pistols, etc.

"Alex, I hear you are pretty good with guns. I think you and Bob should go armed. Since the heavy losses in the Iraqi war, many of the roadblocks are manned by only one or two soldiers. You may be able to shoot your way through and prevent them from warning others of your presence. Take what you feel comfortable with. However I would recommend a couple of Uzis and a couple of pistols with silencers."

189

Alex didn't say anything, but he thought, *I sure have gotten myself into one hell of a mess.* He picked up an Uzi, tested its action, and said, "1'11 take this."

"Good", Felix replied. "I think you should take at least five magazines. These things fire so fast that one burst can use up a magazine in no time."

Alex nodded in agreement. Felix continued, "I like this nine millimeter Sig Sauer Automatic. It fires fifteen rounds and has real stopping power. Also it uses the same ammunition as the Uzis."

McClelland took an Uzi and a Sig Sauer. Patricia decided she would only take a Colt .32, which was small and could be easily concealed.

"Before we go back", Felix said, "Here is a duffle bag for the guns. I would not tell the others that you are armed. There is no point to their knowing this. If they happen to be caught, they may be forced to reveal this, and it would take away any edge you may have."

With that he stuffed the firearms in several old duffle bags and said, "Let's go back in with the rest. On your way out you can put these duffle bags with the rest of your luggage."

Felix held up his hand. "Before you go back there is one more thing."

Felix laid an Uzi on the table and turned to Alex, "I have something here for you. I don't think you're going to like it, but I think you should take it." With that Felix picked up a leather belt. "Watch this," said

Escape from Iran

Felix, pressing on two sides of what appeared to be a solid buckle. The buckle came apart, revealing a small cavity. "This will contain a cyanide pill. I don't think you're going to have to use it, but we're giving you this as a precaution. You do not want the Iranians to catch you."

Alex was absolutely horrified. "My God, Felix, what have you gotten us into?" he shouted in a somewhat shaky and high-pitched voice.

Felix ignored Alex's outburst and picked up a Snickers candy bar. He removed the wrapper and held the candy bar up for Alex and the others to see. He then said, "If you look carefully, this is nothing more than a candy bar. However, if you look closely at the chocolate on the top of the candy bar, you will see the chocolate has a small circle: at one end. Turn over the bar and look on the bottom side and you will see a star, which appears to be part of a trademark at one end. The end with the circle contains poison. Take one bite of it and you're almost instantly dead. The other end is nothing more than a candy bar. You can use this candy bar the same as the pill, if you are in desperate trouble. Also if you're captured, you can offer a candy bar or a bite to your captor. Just be careful when you take a bite that you do not take it out of the end with the circle. I think this is very ingenious. It can be used both to save you from torture or to help you to escape, if you have an opportunity to use it as a weapon."

G. Gray Garland

Alex thought, *I'll never eat another Snickers Bar as long as I live. Oh my God, on second thought I hope I live. Oh Lord, please get me out of this mess.*

Felix looked at the three shocked bystanders and shrugged, "I'm not giving pills to the Ayatollah and Reza. I am afraid it might just spook them."

Felix picked up a Snickers bar and bite into it. The three of them watched in horror.

Felix shrugged, "Don't worry. I bit the good end to show you there is no danger, if you bite the correct end. I am not going to demonstrate what happens if I bite the other end." With that he casually wrapped the end of the bar in a piece of paper and threw it into a wastepaper basket.

Patricia and McClelland watched in shocked silence.

Felix took several more candy bars out of a Snickers box and handed them to Alex. He then took some more and gave them to Patricia and to McClelland. Alex found his hands shaking.

Felix said, "Looking at the lot of you, I think you can all use a strong drink."

No one replied, but they all followed Felix into the pantry of the suite where he made drinks for each of them.

Alex gulped his drink down quickly and held up his glass for a refill. He thought, *We are only sacrificial lambs. All they want is the Ayatollah.*

Nothing else matters to them. We can't go back, and I'm terrified about going on. I only wish I was back at my farm, driving my jeep on my way to the hardware store with Jeremiah in the back. I don't need this. Why did I ever let them talk me into this?

When they returned to the office Felix said, "Okay, now one last word. Be careful and follow your instructions and everything will work out fine. If on the other hand things don't work out and you are caught, you will not be treated kindly. That is the reason I gave each one of you a cyanide pill. If you believe that you are in imminent danger of being caught, you should put it in your mouth. One bite on it and you are dead in an instant without pain. Do what you want with the pills, but I wouldn't want to be caught by the Iranians if I were any of you. Another thing, don't come back here. If you do not reach your destination, I will have to assume that you have been caught and that this place is too dangerous for me. I'll not be here."

Alex could see through a crack in the Venetian blinds that it was still dark outside "I wish this were over and done with. I wish it were 8:00 a,m.".

Felix droned on. Alex half heard him. "Remember you are not necessarily in enemy territory. About half the people were loyal to the Shah and hate the Ayatollah Marzai and his gang. A good number of the remaining people do not like the present regime, so people, your odds of getting out are pretty good."

Alex thought, *Probably exaggerated, but with some semblance of truth.*

CHAPTER 38

The wait was almost unbearable. Dawn finally came. The day was cold and windy, but there was no sign of the rain or snow that had been expected.

Felix left the safe house at around seven thirty to make sure that the cars were in place.

He returned shortly after eight and told them everything was ready. He again went over the maps that he had previously shown them. Patricia, the ayatollah, and the ayatollah's daughter would use the faded blue, Chevrolet sedan, and Alex and McClelland would follow in the Toyota Land Rover.

He handed the keys and papers for the Chevrolet to Patricia.

"Good Luck. At this time of day there'll be a lot of traffic. No one will notice you. Drive carefully and remember to go slowly until you receive the signal from Alex that he is behind you."

He was referring to a prearranged signal. Alex would tap his walkie-talkier three times to indicate that he and McClelland were in

Escape from Iran

the Toyota and underway without any problems. If all was okay with Patricia, she was to acknowledge with four quick taps on her walkie talkie. There was also a code for various types of trouble. For example, being stopped by the police or military or approaching a road block would be two quick taps followed momentarily by two more taps.

Felix once again checked their Iranian clothing. "Okay. Patricia let's go."

With that Patricia, the Ayatollah and his daughter followed Felix to the back stairway. Alex thought that Patricia gave him a rather woeful look as she left.

It seemed like a long time, but in fact, it was only a few minutes before Felix returned and said, "Okay Alex you and Bob can go."

As they left the building and walked into the alley, Alex felt exposed and vulnerable. He couldn't speak the language, and he didn't really know where he was or where he was going, although he had been shown his first destination on a map.

When they reached the street it was busy with the hustle and bustle of people going to work. Alex was comforted by the fact that no one appeared to be paying any attention to Bob or him. They walked the short distance to the Toyota without incident. There were no policemen or soldiers in sight. Alex got into the driver's seat. It had been decided that Alex would drive and Bob would give directions, because it had been sometime since Bob had driven a car. Everywhere he went he had been driven by his chauffeurs.

Bob tapped the walkie-talkie mike three times. It seemed like ages before Patricia answered that she was on her way and everything was okay. They were off and running.

On hearing that Bob and Alex were behind her Patricia increased her speed to that of the traffic around her, as directed by Felix. She thought, *I wonder if I can pass muster if we are stopped.* She had been taught a few phrases in Parsee, so that she could answer a request to show her papers or answer some simple questions. She would have to rely on the ayatollah or his daughter, and she would not be able to understand what they were saying. That made her very apprehensive.

As they left the center of the city, traffic was not so heavy, but she was surprised at the number of cars on the streets. Many of them were old and beat up like her Chevrolet. She thought she could see the Toyota Land Rover following about a quarter of a mile behind from time to time.

As they left the city, they came upon their first roadblock. She noticed the cars in front of her slowing down to show their identification papers.

She began to slow down and tapped her walkie-talkie before putting it back in its hiding place. Much to her surprise, as each car in front of her slowed down, the guards merely waved it through the

Escape from Iran

barricade. *Are these commuters that the guards know because they came through everyday?"* she wondered as she slowed down. To her surprise the guard hardly looked at them and waved them through. She let out a sigh of relief and took out the walkie-talkie to give the signal that they had gotten through okay.

Her disguise had passed at least this roadblock. Because women were not allowed to drive automobiles in Iran, she had been disguised to look like a man. Felix had even given her some make up to make it look like she had a black shadow of stubble of someone who had to shave everyday.

Alex's Toyota reached the roadblock with McClelland playing the sleeping commuter. The guard motioned for the vehicle to slow down, seemed to glance into it, and then waved it on. They too had passed the first roadblock.

The further they went away from the city the fewer cars they encountered. After about fifty miles they were almost the only cars on the road. Alex continued to follow the Chevrolet about a quarter to half mile behind it, and the two cars were frequently in sight of each other on the level straightaway.

For the next several hours they drove on without encountering any additional roadblocks. As the distance from Tehran increased the traffic thinned considerably. There were very few automobiles on the road.

G. Gray Garland

Most of the traffic consisted of an occasional truck They encountered no military or police vehicles.

Patricia tapped her microphone to indicate she wanted to stop. Alex acknowledged her signal with a tap, and the two cars turned onto a side road and drove about fifty yards to a grove of trees where they pulled off the road. When Alex got out of the Toyota, he could hear the sound of a vehicle or vehicles moving at a very rapid rate on the main highway. He walked several feet to a spot where he had a pretty good view of the highway without being seen.

Within a few moments he saw what he had heard. Two army vehicles, a Jeep followed by a weapons carrier, were moving very fast in the direction Alex's group had been traveling. His stomach tightened. He wondered if the Iranians were on to them. He walked down the rise to join the others. The sight of the fast moving military vehicles made Alex very apprehensive, but he decided not to say anything to the others. It would be too dangerous to turn back now, and there was nothing to gain by unduly worrying the others. He decided instead to suggest that he and McClelland take the lead for a while. He walked down to where the vehicles were parked. Patricia and McClelland were standing by the open tailgate of the Toyota drinking coffee and eating sandwiches, which they had brought from the safe house. The ayatollah and his daughter were off to the side, more or less staring into space.

Escape from Iran

McClelland said, "It's getting pretty cool. I suggest we eat up and get underway as soon as possible, if we want to reach the barn near Chardeh before dark.

Patricia said that the ayatollah's daughter had to go to the bathroom. The two girls went behind some bushes.

A few minutes later they were underway with Alex and McClelland in the lead. For several hours they drove north without incident. Alex was beginning to relax a little. He had almost forgotten the speeding military vehicles. They probably were on their way to some local problem.

The roads were now two lanes, narrow, pitted, and somewhat twisting. They were very poor by U.S. standards, even for a country road.

As the Toyota descended a hill which sloped to their right the road, became quite narrow. Alex could see the mountains in the distance on his left, but the hill blocked any view to the right. They rounded a curve and Alex's heart skipped a beat. Positioned across the road were the two military vehicles he had seen earlier. He could not turn around. The road was too narrow. And even if he did turn around, he would arouse the suspicions of the soldiers at the roadblock.

"Tap the Walkie-Talkie. Warn Patricia," Alex said calmly to McClelland. He did not feel very calm. In fact he was quite scared.

McClelland, who had been half-dozing, was fully alert in an instant.

"Let me do the talking. I speak Farsi"

"OK, but put the Uzi under your robe", said Alex, checking his Sig Sauer to make certain there was a shell in its chamber and then carefully placing it under some oily rags on the floor.

Alex slowed down and came to stop at the roadblock. There were a number of soldiers lounging around a small fire, smoking and drinking coffee, but only one came over to the Toyota. McClelland, with his disguise, including a large mustache, which Felix had given to him, really looked like a typical Iranian, He had their papers in his hand ready to show them to the soldier, but the soldier merely looked into the Toyota and waved them through.

Alex and McClelland both let out a sigh of relief. "I cannot believe how easy that was," said McClelland wiping the perspiration from his forehead.

They were just beginning to relax when they heard four taps on their walkie-talkie. Patricia's group was in trouble.

CHAPTER 39

"We've got to go back and help them", said Alex.

"Yes, I guess so." replied McClelland somewhat dejectedly.

Alex found a wide spot in the road and turned the Toyota around.

"The roadblock is around the next curve", Alex said

"One of us should get out of the car and go over the hill and cover the other one in the car. I'll go over the hill, and you can drive the car. You speak Farsi. and I don't. When I get to the point where I can see or cover the roadblock I'll wave to you. Then you can drive the Toyota around the curve. Slow down like you are going to stop for the roadblock. Then when you are close enough floor it, and run over as many of them as you can. In the meantime I'll be coming down the hill, and I'll try to take out as many as I can with the Uzi."

"1 think the roadblock is around the next curve", repeated Alex, slowing the Toyota to a stop. Alex got out picked up his Uzi and his canvas bag containing the extra clips of ammo.

"Wait until I signal you. There is a chance they may be letting them through. If so, I will give you thumbs up. If not, I will give you thumbs down. If I wave my arms up and down quickly, it will mean get in fast."

McClelland nodded and moved into the driver's seat placing his Uzi and his pistol on the passenger seat. Alex scrambled up the bank. He had removed his robes, but even so he found it very difficult to go very fast.

He finally reached a point where he felt he could see the roadblock and not be seen. The roadblock was about fifty yards below him. He could see the ayatollah standing to one side and holding his daughter, who appeared to be weeping. Patricia had been pushed back onto the hood of the Jeep. A soldier held each of her arms while another appeared to be either interrogating or torturing her. Her blouse had been torn away, and she was bare breasted.

Alex could not help but think, *What a great set.*

After refocusing Alex thought, *If McClelland can divert them long enough, I can probably get down the slope to a position where I can fire with some accuracy.* He noticed some rocks about ten yards below and thought, *If I can get down to those rocks, I should have a pretty good field of fire, and I can rest my Uzi on top of the rocks.*

Escape from Iran

He carefully moved around the hill and signaled to McClelland waving his arm up and down rapidly. McClelland, weakly waved his left arm back.

The soldiers either heard or saw the Toyota coming. Two of them moved to man the roadblock while the other three moved quickly to get their prisoners out of sight.

Alex slid quickly down the hill to his firing position behind a large boulder. He peeped around the boulder. Several of the soldiers were coming in his direction, but they had not seen him. They were looking in the direction of the Toyota.

The officer was pulling Patricia by her arm, and he was followed a step or two behind by one of soldiers. The ayatollah and his daughter were walking by themselves followed by another soldier, who was halfheartedly prodding them with an AK-47. Alex surmised that if he could time it right, and he was not seen too soon, he could take out the officer without hitting Patricia and swing on the other two soldiers before they could fire at him.

They came near to where Alex crouched. Instead of looking in his direction they were still looking back at the Toyota, which was now approaching the roadblock. Alex rested the Uzi on the rock, aimed at the captain's head and fired several rounds. The captain's head dissolved into a bloody puff, but by that time Alex was swinging to aim at the other two soldiers. Two quick bursts took them out before they could recover from their surprise and fire a shot. Alex then scrambled down toward the roadblock.

The two soldiers manning the roadblock upon hearing Alex's shots had turned in his direction. Alex watched with fascinated horror as McClelland floored the Toyota. There was a sickening thump as the Toyota hit the first soldier. The second soldier had scrambled out of the way, but he was so shocked he did not know which way to run. Even though he was about 20 yards away, Alex cut him down with a burst from his Uzi.

CHAPTER 40

For several moments everyone was too stunned to say anything. Finally McClelland walked over from the Toyota and said, "Let's get the hell out of here."

Alex, reloading his Uzi, "Not so fast. How are you Patricia?"

"I am OK," she replied buttoning her blouse and pulling her robe around her. "They just roughed me up a little bit. Who knows what they would have done, if you hadn't come back."

"I think we ought to clean this mess up and get the hell out of here," said Alex.

"What do you mean, 'Clean up this mess!' We've got to get moving ," said a shaking McClelland

"If we leave everything here, someone will come along and know what happened. It will create a massive manhunt. We've got to hide the vehicles and the bodies. We'd better hurry before someone comes along and sees this mess. If that happens, we are in real trouble," repeated Alex.

McClelland in a shaky voice said, "Let's just dump the cars and run. We'll be a long way away before they figure it was us, if they ever do."

"No, I think I have a better idea", said Patricia. "If they are looking for us, they are probably looking for five people. That's why we decided to go in two cars. The only one shot in the face is the captain. Let's take their vehicles and prop up the other bodies as passengers, two in the back seat of the Jeep and two in the weapons carrier. Bob speaks Farsi, so he can wear the captain's uniform."

"Bob, take the captain's uniform and put it on", said Alex, ignoring McClelland's protest that he did not want to put on the captain's bloody uniform.

"I'll dress in one of the soldier's uniforms. Patricia, you pull those vehicles off the road, so that if someone comes along, it doesn't look like a roadblock," Alex ordered.

"But Alex if we put on these uniforms and are caught we will be shot as spies," countered McClelland.

"We'll probably be shot or worse no matter what. Let's get moving," replied Alex.

"Better yet," interrupted Alex. "Let's all go in the weapons carrier. Bob and I in the front seat. I'll drive. We will put the three soldiers and you in the back."

"Why three, Alex?" Patricia said.

Escape from Iran

Alex replied. "I am going to need the uniform of one of them, if I sit in the front and drive. We were lucky this time. I think we have a better chance if we are all together when we hit a roadblock. If we have a problem, Bob and I can fire from the front and you can fire from the back.

McClelland spoke up, "These Iranian vehicles may not be in the best of shape. Remember now they haven't been able to get parts for a long time. At least we know our vehicles are in pretty good shape. I vote that we take the weapons carrier and our Toyota. Alex can drive the weapons carrier and I can ride shotgun with the Ayatollah and his daughter, and the soldiers can ride in the rear of the weapons carrier. Patricia can drive the Toyota. We will put her in a uniform. On second thought, forget taking the dead soldiers."

"You're probably right. We don't want to be caught with the dead soldiers. We'd never be able to talk our way out of that!" said Alex.

Patricia moved the two army vehicles to the side of the road.

The ayatollah and his daughter stood off to one side, still bewildered and shocked by what had gone on.

Alex and McClelland undressed the dead soldiers and put on their uniforms. Alex felt a little nauseated. The corpses were pretty bloody, especially the captain's, who had been shot in the head.

'Patricia, you have to get into one of these uniforms too. Okay, now let's strip the Chevy of anything we might need and put it in the weapons carrier. Be sure you get all the gas cans. About 50 yards down the road there is a ravine. I'll take the Jeep down there and push it off the hillside.

"Bob, you and Patricia pull the hood up on the Chevy, so it will look like it broke down. Pull some wires and disable it, so it can't be used. Be sure you get everything out of it that would enable anyone to tie it to us."

"What are we going to do with these bodies? We can't leave them here," said Patricia.

"Load them in the Jeep," said Alex.

It took all three,-Alex, Bob and Patricia,-to load them in the Jeep.

Alex then got in and drove it to the edge of the road by the ravine, got out, and pushed it down the slope. The Jeep bounced down the hill a short distance and was stopped by some boulders.

"It's not what I had hoped for, but at least it is out of sight of anyone driving along the road," thought Alex.

Alex went back to join the others. Patricia was dressed in a soldier's uniform and was loading gear from the Chevy into the weapons carrier. McClelland looked almost as shocked as the ayatollah and his daughter, but he was also storing gear in the weapons carrier.

The Chevy was disabled and pushed down into the ravine where it could not be seen from the road. They were quickly on their way.

Escape from Iran

Alex drove the weapons carrier with McClelland sitting beside him dressed as an Iranian officer. The ayatollah and his daughter were in the back of the weapons carrier. Patricia followed alone, driving the Toyota. Alex hated to leave her by herself, but he wanted McClelland with him. If they were stopped at another roadblock, he needed an "officer" who spoke Farsi. They continued driving encountering only an occasional vehicle.

There were no roadblocks.

Alex noticed that the weapons carrier had a two-way Motorola radio. *Just like the one I have in my car at home"* he thought.

For the most part the radio was quiet. There were occasional transmissions. Alex could not understand what was being said, but McClelland assured him that the messages were very routine.

Apparently no one was looking for them.

Alex had a map that had been given to him by Felix. This map itself was not marked, but there was an overlay to the map showing a false escape route into Turkey, which was marked with a number of red and blue dots. By measuring the distances between the designated red and blue dots it was possible to obtain the coordinates to use on the unmarked map, enabling them to easily locate the hideaway to which they were going.

Felix had briefed them on what to look for, so Alex and McClelland knew they were to look for an old deserted barn.

209

It was beginning to get dark and Alex was beginning to be very apprehensive when they found the road about which Felix had told them. He drove about three quarters of a mile and there before them was the barn.

The barn appeared deserted. Nearby were the ruins of a farmhouse. It appeared that the farmhouse must have been destroyed by fire some years ago. The yard was overgrown. They opened the barn doors with little effort and drove the weapons carrier and the Toyota into the barn and closed the doors. The barn appeared to be clean inside. Felix must have been there. After stretching their legs and looking around they unloaded a few things and had a cold supper. They were too tired to do any cooking.

They retired without detailing anyone to stand guard. Alex felt that they were hidden well enough that no one would find them while it was still dark. He set his alarm watch for 6:30 a.m.. It would still be dark, and he would have time enough to look around for any activity before daylight.

The ayatollah and his daughter took one corner, and Alex and McClelland placed their sleeping bags in front of the door. Alex was a light sleeper and he did not want anyone leaving or coming in without his knowing it.

He was about to get into his sleeping bag when Patricia came over and placed her sleeping bag next to his. Do you mind? She said.

Escape from Iran

"No of course not," he replied.

He turned off the lantern, and the barn was in darkness. He felt Patricia climbing into his sleeping bag.

"Just hold me," she said.

She was shivering almost uncontrollably. Alex held her tightly until they both dropped off to sleep from sheer exhaustion.

The next morning Alex turned on the radio in the weapons carrier. The radio was busy. There was a lot of traffic back and forth. Bob said, "They are looking for the weapons carrier and the Jeep. They don't know what happened to them. They only know that the vehicles and soldiers have disappeared. They are sending additional units into the area to look," McClelland continued, "This might be good. They will have a lot of people looking and most of them will not know each other. It might give us just a little better chance."

"I think we should get rid of the weapons carrier." It was Patricia speaking. "They will be looking for the missing army vehicles, so the weapons carrier will draw too much attention. Taking it will be too dangerous. They will not be looking for the Toyota. Also, if they are looking for us, they will be looking for five persons, so we shall have to somehow make it look like we are at least six. We can stuff some luggage into a uniform, put a cap on it, and make it look like a sleeping soldier. In this way we will appear to be party of six or seven, and hopefully they will not pay too much attention to us. We can make them look like they are asleep."

"I think you are right." said Alex. "Let's load everything into the Toyota."

"What about these uniforms. Do we get have to wear them? I don't think those guys ever took a bath. They stink," said McClelland.

"No, I don't think we should keep on the uniforms," countered Alex.

"I agree," replied Patricia.

Alex then said, "Bob, you listen to the radio for awhile, and see if you can get any information, such as where they are concentrating their search. We are fifty or sixty miles," he paused to wipe his forehead, "from the roadblock. Meantime let's see if we can find something in the barn that we can use to hide the weapons carrier in case someone looks in here.

Patricia came back a few minutes later. "Alex there is a pond down at the foot of the hill, and there is a path leading down to it, but it is pretty narrow. However, I think we can get the weapons carrier down the path, if we are careful. I am going to walk down and see how deep the pond is I'll be right back."

What a girl, Alex thought. *After all she went through yesterday I only hope McClelland holds up as well as she is doing.*

Escape from Iran

McClelland reported that the radio messages mostly concerned units being sent south to look for the missing soldiers, their headquarters fearing suspected Iraqi terrorists, but they were puzzled because the Iraqis had never penetrated so far into the interior. Nothing indicated that they were suspected.

Patricia returned to say that the pond seemed to be deep enough to conceal the weapons carrier.

Alex thought aloud, *I wonder if we can take the two-way radio out of the weapons carrier. It sure would be handy to know what was going on. It shouldn't be too hard.* On several occasions he had removed his own radios when he had purchased a new car, but he had never installed one.

It didn't take to long to disconnect and remove the radio. Then he had to install it in the Toyota. He was able to snake the power cable through a hole in the floor board. He attached the antennae wire to the Toyota radio antennae and connected the power cable to the battery. It was somewhat crude, but it seemed to work. It was now about nine-thirty in the morning, so Alex suggested Patricia and the ayatollah's daughter prepare breakfast while he and McClelland disposed of the weapons carrier.

"Bob, wait till I check to see if everything is clear. Then we will take the weapons carrier down to the pond. "

In a moment Alex was back. "Okay, let's go."

213

Alex drove the weapons carrier out of the barn and down the path to the pond. Before he got to the edge, he stopped the weapons carrier and put on the handbrake leaving the car in gear. He put a little additional pressure on the accelerator, checking to make certain that the handbrake would hold the vehicle. He then released the handbrake and drove to the edge of the pond.

"This is the end of the line," he said to McClelland, who got out of the car. Alex backed the car up ten feet or more, put the car in low gear, pulled the handbrake on and got out. As soon as he released the hand brake, the weapons carrier moved slowly forward, picking up enough momentum to go over the embankment and into the pond where it slowly sunk out of sight.

Alex turned to Bob, "Before we leave we are going to have to wash the Toyota. It is so dirty from the muddy roads that it will attract attention. A keen observer would know we've come from the south. The roads here are a lot cleaner, and I noticed that the cars we have encountered here are not so dirty. Let's wash it. We don't have to do too good of a job, because if it is too clean, it will also attract attention, but I think we have to get some of the mud off it before we leave."

It took a lot longer than Alex had hoped to wash the car. They had to be careful not to do a good job. Alex did not want the car to look too clean. They had to bring water up from the pond. However, in a little more than an hour they were again underway. They were very crowded, but glad to be moving again.

CHAPTER 41

It had been five days since the Ayatollah Montazeri had disappeared. Majid paced up and down in his office, chain smoking Marlboros and thinking, *Where could they be? I don't think they're out of the Country. If they were, the Americans would have made a big event of it. They can't keep anything quiet. They must brag to the world. There's been no news. They must still be here.*

None of our searches have revealed a trace of them. I just do not believe McClelland is involved. His disappearance may just be a coincidence. Or is it? No, it's not a coincidence. Blair was staying with him, and they both disappeared. No, he's in it up to his ears too. I knew letting this Blair in was wrong. I sensed trouble from the very beginning. The Iman should have listened to me. What have we missed. We've checked the roadblocks to the West. No sign, but the soldiers are so young and sloppy. They could have gotten through without it being reported. No, they are still here. But where?

G. Gray Garland

What would I do? I'd go into Turkey or maybe Russia. But that's not possible. We've warned the Russians that there will be trouble, if they let them into Russia. Yet, I don't trust the Russkys. They might allow them to sneak through. Probably not, but maybe I should check that. Russia. Hmm. I wonder if the strange killing of the soldiers at the roadblock near Incheh could be related. If you were going to escape through Russia, you would probably go on that road.

He pushed his intercom button. "Hassam! Come here on the double."

A young major entered the office, came stiffly to attention and saluted. "Yes, General?"

"I want you to take a helicopter and fly up to Incheh and check out what happened at that roadblock where the soldiers were killed and the military vehicles stolen. You know, we thought it was Iraqi commandos, but that doesn't make sense. There was no sabotage in the area. It could be Blair's group.

"Check on records of cars that went through. They're supposed to log all vehicles. You and I know some of them are too sloppy and too lazy to keep records, but we may just be lucky one of these times. Check for witnesses, if possible. Ask around. See if any of the vehicles were spotted with unusual passengers."

"That may be difficult," replied the young officer. "All of our military vehicles are all alike."

Escape from Iran

"Try anyway." Majid snapped.

"Take Sergeant Manieh and Lieutenant Leylaz with you. You may need help. Don't hesitate to requisition any help you need from the locals."

"Yes, General."

"Also check the roadblocks before Incheh and the roadblocks after Incheh.

"We can compare the sheets, and maybe we can find a car going towards the border that will give us a clue. Keep me informed at least twice a day. Do you understand?"

"Yes. General."

When he finished talking with his young aide, Majid again pressed the intercom button on his desk and requested his secretary to summon all of the officers of A Section to an immediate meeting in his conference room.

He knew that a number of them were out of the office for one reason or another, but there would be more than enough of them for what he wanted.

When they had assembled in his conference room he addressed them. "We have a major problem on our hands. An American, named McClelland, who has lived here for many years invited an old friend of his from America, named Blair, to visit him. This was done with the permission of the Ayatollah. I might add much against my advice.

217

McClelland and Blair have disappeared together with the ayatollah Montarzeri and his daughter. We must find them before they leave the country. Both McClelland and the Ayatollah Montarzeri have information, which could be very damaging to the security of our country, especially if the Americans were able to obtain this information. This is to be given your undivided attention. This means all of you. Do you understand?"

This was followed by a chorus of "Yes Sirs."

"Azari, I want you to get on the telephone and call every frontier post in the area, and especially to the north of Incheh. I want you to check with them to see if anyone answering the description I am going to give you has crossed the border within the last six days. Use my name and authority. If you have any problems, get back to me immediately, and I'll take care of them. This is most urgent. Put everything else aside. Do this now and get back to me as soon as you know something."

"Tabar, I want you and Shadi to report back to me as soon as you can with maps of the Incheh area and the border north. Ali, I want you to get in touch with the Army and requisition four or five helicopters together with pilots. Unless we hear that McClelland's party has crossed into Russia, I want the helicopters to start patrolling along our border with Russia immediately."

Escape from Iran

The young aide to whom he was speaking spoke, "Sir, do you want the helicopters to start immediately or do you want them to wait until you give the word?"

Majid angrily slammed his hand down on the conference room table, so hard that his half smoked cigarette bounced out of the ashtray. "Didn't you understand me? I said "Immediately." I want them to start immediately. As the Americans say, 'Time is of the essence.' If they have already crossed, we can always stand down. However I would hate to have them cross over while we held the helicopters back while waiting word. Get them in the air immediately. Now means now!"

"Yes, Sir."

"Hallizf, I want you to contact the police in the Aydere area and find out from them the logical places that a fugitive might use to cross over, places that a smuggler might have used. Go with Tabar and Shadi and get a copy of the map we are going to use. Mark these places on the map and report back here as soon as you can.

If any of you are working on something that you feel is too urgent for you to leave, give it to Hallizt. If he can't handle it, he should report to me for instructions. OK, get going."

As they began to file out of the conference room, Majid said, "Hamid stay here a minute. He paused to light another Marlboro, ignoring the half- smoked cigarette in the ash tray in front of him.

G. Gray Garland

"I want you to keep track of the equipment and manpower. I want to know at all times where all the helicopters and ground units are so that we can move them to the right place quickly. Let me know how many people we have available. If we need more, I'll contact the army. I'm going to catch those bastards, if it's the last thing I ever do."

CHAPTER 42

It was relatively easy. The military helicopter followed the main road from Tehran to Inchen, landing at each roadblock. The two officers would check the records and talk to the soldiers on duty. It was very discouraging. The records were sloppy and their memories were vague. There was nothing to indicate that McClelland's party had fled north.

They landed at the roadblock where the shoot out had occurred. A new contingent of soldiers had replaced those who had been killed. The new soldiers were very alert and their records were very well maintained, but they had no knowledge of what had gone on before they had replaced the soldiers who were killed. If any old records had been found, they were likely at the local command post.

It was at the next roadblock that they found their first clue. One of the soldiers remembered a weapons carrier that had passed through. There were two men in uniform and two Iranians in the rear. That wasn't so unusual, but the weapons carrier was followed by a white Toyota Station Wagon, which was also driven by a soldier. The Toyota was very dirty, appearing as if it had been on a long and dirty trip. It didn't feel right to him, but he was not about to challenge the Iranian captain sitting in the drivers seat.

This could be it", thought the young lieutenant from Majid's office. He could not wait to call headquarters. He walked briskly to the nearest jeep, picked up the microphone and requested that he be patched through to Tehran.

When Majid heard this he said, "Lieutenant, check the next road block and report back to me."

"But, General, there are no more road blocks between here and the border. The next check point will be at the border crossing."

"When did they pass through the roadblock?" snapped Majid.

Lieutenant Leylaz nervously replied," One, maybe two days ago I'll have to check again."

Majid had a sinking feeling. We may be too late. I'll hang on while you give me the exact time and date."

After a minute or two the Lieutenant again picked up the microphone. "They passed through yesterday."

"We may be too late. Check with the border control people and get back to me immediately I'll not leave the office until you let me know what they say"

Escape from Iran

"Yes sir."

Less than ten miles away McClelland, who was monitoring the military frequency, could hardly believe what he had just heard.

CHAPTER 43

It was dark by the time they reached the border between Iran and Russia. Even with Felix's maps they had gotten lost three times.

Alex was relieved when he at last drove the Toyota off the trail and behind a clump of bushes to hide it from anyone going by.

They were now in mountainous country. It was rocky, and it was very cold.

"I think we should stay pretty close to the car tonight. It's too rocky to do much exploring. Someone may fall and get hurt. We can build a fire under that ledge. It faces away from the trail, so it will not be seen from the road. We can cook some supper and then get a good nights sleep."

A fire was lighted, but the warmth did little to raise their spirits. Dinner was eaten in silence. All of them appeared to be wrapped up in their own thoughts.

The Ayatollah appeared unusually solemn and unhappy. This made Alex uneasy. *I wonder if he is having second thoughts. If he got up in*

224

the middle of the night and went back, he could always claim that we kidnapped him, and he escaped. He could then turn us in before we got across the border. Boy what a mess. I must not let my thoughts get too negative. The ayatollah spoke fairly fluent English. However, he seldom said anything to anyone. Alex wondered what he was thinking. "Are you okay?" said Alex. The ayatollah merely nodded.

"I'm going to walk up the trail a few hundred yards. I don't want to wake up in the middle of the night and find we are in the middle of an army camp. Patricia, would you like to come along with me?"

With that he put his radio in his left pocket and his pistol in his right pocket, picked up a flashlight, and then he and Patricia started up what appeared to be a trail.

Alex thought it might be safe to use his radio. It was not the scheduled time for making a transmission, but he hoped that someone might be listening. He turned on the radio, and after aiming it for several seconds in the direction of where there might be a satellite, the green light came on and was steady. He had found a receptive satellite. He entered a message. Then he pressed the transmit button and sent a burst transmission. Much to his surprise within a few seconds the screen on his radio lit up with a text message.

"Do not cross border into Russia. Repeat. Do not attempt to return through Russia. Russians have reneged on our agreement.

KGB has orders to detain you and McClelland. This could be fatal."

Alex scrolled through the message on the screen of his radio again for the third time. His stomach churned, and, in spite of the cold weather, he began to sweat. He showed the message to Patricia.

Alex thought to himself, *How could I have gotten into this mess! Good God. What a terrible mess they've left us in. This may mean death or torture for all of us. How could they do this to us? We were lucky to be able to get this far. Now what will we do. We can't backtrack.*

When he saved the message on the screen he noticed that his hands were shaking.

"My God, Patricia, to get this far and have the rug pulled out from under us."

Patricia stared at him. She had read the message. She knew the message was bad news. He handed the radio to her and walked to the other side of the hill and looked across the valley. The lights twinkling in the distance were in Russia, the village of Megin.

"Maybe we should ignore the radio signals and go on into Russia anyway."

Patricia joined him. All she said was, "My God, how could they do this to us." They stared across the valley in silence.

Escape from Iran

"Let's not tell the others until we decide what we are going to do," said Patricia. "Maybe they'll have another plan when they broadcast the next transmission. When is the next transmission? Do you know?"

Alex looked at his watch and computed the time in his head. "The message will come in sometime between 8:20 and 8:30 tomorrow morning."

Patricia looked at her watch and said, "That's about nine hours and 15 minutes. We should have our map ready in case they do suggest an alternate location."

Alex nodded. "That's a good idea."

In the morning when they received an answer it was, "No alternate plan ready, will contact you tomorrow at 11:12 our time", which Alex decided it meant they really had no back-up plan.

CHAPTER 44

Since receiving the message telling them not to enter Russia, Alex had checked in with his radio again later the next day, but there were no instructions for him. It was very discouraging. They were cold and running low on food.

On the morning of the third day they heard a car laboring up the trail.

With weapons ready they peeped around the rocks to see who was coming. An old truck, rusty and dented all over came around the bend. Its only occupant, the driver, was a rather grungy Iranian sporting a large mustache with the handlebars turned down. The truck turned off the trail and went around the bushes toward where the Toyota was hidden.

Alex flipped off the safety and raised his Uzi. Out of the corner of his eye he could see that Bob and Patricia had done the same. They were all nervously fingering the triggers of their firearms.

Escape from Iran

The occupant of the truck got out of the truck very slowly, making certain at all times that his hands were in full view.

This doesn't add up, thought Alex, something is definitely not right.

Facing them the truck driver slowly took off his hat and dropped it at his side. Next to the utter surprise of those watching, he took off a large bushy wig and dropped it. He then pulled off his handlebar mustache.

It was Felix!

CHAPTER 45

In Washington, D.C. it was about three o'clock in the morning. Word that Blair and McClelland with the Ayatollah and his daughter were on the run towards Russia had reached Langley. The director, when he received word about midnight, had called for an emergency meeting at 2:00 a.m. in his conference room. He was very apprehensive. On the one hand the plan seemed to be working. On the other hand they still had to get them out of Iran. And he had ordered that they not go out through Russia.

Robert Gordon had great confidence in Felix, but they were not out of Iran yet.

The Operation Fishhook group had all been awakened and told to report at once. They had been there for several hours trying to figure out what they could do to solve this dilemma. The conference room was littered with fast-food boxes and half-filled coffee cups. There was a large map of Iran and the surrounding areas pinned to a board mounted on the wall. A blackboard was covered with a garble mess of

Escape from Iran

figures and arrows. The director, who was normally very fastidious, had removed his coat, pulled down his tie and opened his shirt collar. The rest of the six men, who were either sitting at the table or pacing nearby were all pretty much equally informal and somewhat weary looking.

Present were the director, the assistant director, the director of covert operations, Mike Hogan, John Eppes from Communications, Mohamed Azar, the Iranian specialist from the training facility in Virginia, and Robert Gordon, who had arrived late, having been summoned from Chicago. Rose Mitchell, the director's secretary was also present, sometimes taking notes and sometimes filling coffee cups from the percolator on the sideboard.

"There is just no way we can send in any helicopters or planes to rescue them. From what we know about where they are, we would have to go in from Russia. As we all know, that would be impossible. The Russians would never allow us to do that," said Mike Hogan.

"Do you think we can ask the president to ask the Russians to let them cross the border into Russia?" interjected Sampson.

"Absolutely not," replied Cabot. The president has said they can not go into Russia, *I know this isn't true, another lie by me, but if I asked the president, he would fire me without another thought. I would be screwed, especially if I was bringing out McClelland and everyone would know I lied when I said I had obtained immunity for him.*

"I guess at this point all we can do is pray that by some miracle they do get out," said the very tired looking Cabot, who thought at the same time, *What will happen to me, if McClelland comes back saying he was promised immunity.*

Dawn was breaking outside the conference room windows. It looked like a gloomy day. "Gentlemen, I guess that's all we can do today. Go home and get some sleep. Maybe tomorrow will know more or have some ideas. In any event, if I need you, I'll call you."

CHAPTER 46

The euphoria of Felix's arrival was quickly dissipated when Felix informed them that the Russians had not changed their position. They did not want the ayatollah to enter the Soviet Union.

"What are we going to do?" asked McClelland looking more dejected and miserable than Alex had ever seen him look.

"To try to go back across Iran to the Turkish border would be very risky." Felix replied. "We are still going out through Russia."

"I don't understand", replied Alex.

"Well, the way I figure it, you can't stay here. Sooner or later you will get caught. The Iranians are fanatics. It's a religious thing with them. Few, if any, would give you shelter or hide you. Even if they wanted to, they would be afraid. Someone would report them, and then they would be in terrible trouble. You can't stay here. You can't stay camped out here. Both of you are now coughing and sneezing. You would develop pneumonia and die."

Felix continued, "I figure it this way. If we can get into Russia, even if you are caught, the chances are the Russians would not hold you for very long. They probably would let us take the ayatollah out of Russia, providing we promised not to say that he escaped through Russia. It is a hot potato for them. They will want to get rid of it as fast as they can. Our problem will be getting into Russia. Getting out of Iran should not be too tough. The Iranians are pretty sloppy in this area. I guess for one reason, no one really wants to go from here to Russia, and for a second reason the Russians certainly don't want to come here."

"From the top of this mountain you get a great view of the border. In fact, on a clear day you can see for quite some distance. Tomorrow, as soon as it is light, we will go up to the top of the mountain and check things out."

Before they had gotten over their surprise at Felix's arrival and his statement that they were going into Russia, Felix said, "I brought you food and drink, so don't look so down and out."

Out of the frying pan and into the fire, thought Alex. *But then again, maybe the Russians would probably not torture and kill us as would the Iranians.*

CHAPTER 47

Lieutenant Leylaz spoke into the microphone from his helicopter. "Sir, there is no evidence whatsoever of anyone resembling McClelland's party crossing into Russia. The border guards' records are quite good. I don't think they could have gotten across the border without our knowing it.

The last trace of them, if you could even call it that, was the roadblock near Inchehen where the weapons carrier and the Toyota Station Wagon went through together-or at least the guard thought they were together. Now maybe they were able to cross the border using some trail in the mountains, but they would still have to get across the river. I don't think they could do this without help from the Russians or someone on the other side of the river, maybe the CIA.

Suddenly Majid interrupted the Lieutenant. "Wait a minute. I remember when I was a young boy there were rumors that the Americans had a crossing point near Gifan. One of my neighbors was with the border police. I remember him saying he thought the Americans sent

G. Gray Garland

agents into Russia at a crossing point near his post. This was during the Shah's time when the bloody Americans controlled Iran. His unit would be pulled away from that area, and he would see American automobiles containing Americans or at least American types drive by.

Majid continued, "I want you to go to the village of Gifan. It's close to the border with Russia. Talk only to Captain Wadeh. He is our man, and he will keep anything you tell him confidential. Find out from him whether Old Borsehi is still alive. If he is, he probably still lives on Kurat Street. No one from that village ever moves.

"Wait at the station until you hear from me. Don't talk to anyone else. Don't use the phones. A lot of the people up there don't like the government. They don't like any government. They would be glad to help the McClelland party merely because he was running from the police.

"When I hang up I am going to start up there. Stay at the police station. I'll contact you there, but when I do, do not use names. Just say you found the person you were looking for. When I get there I'll give you further instructions."

"Yes sir. "

Majid immediately called the ayatollah at Quom. He was unable to get through to the Ayatollah, but he talked with one of his chief aides, Ayatollah Mossein, who assured Majid that the matter would be given top priority. He would immediately notify General Hamid to

Escape from Iran

make available to Majid any army equipment or personnel he might require.

Majid called one of his aides into his office He explained to him that he would need at least six helicopters and one thousand men to patrol the border near Gifan, so that the McClelland party could not escape. They should be armed and equipped to operate in the mountainous territory along the Iran-Russian Border.

The rotors of Majid's helicopter were already turning as he left the office and trotted out to the landing pad. He climbed into the helicopter and buckled himself into the seat beside the pilot.

"Take me to Hanger Seven at the military airport. There should be a Learjet waiting for me there. After you drop me off, I want you to refuel and proceed to the military airport at Shirvan and await further orders.

Majid was on his way.

CHAPTER 48

The next morning they all awoke cold and stiff. During the night the temperature had fallen well below the freezing mark. The fire had died during the night, and there was a light coating of snow on the ground.

Once they were up and moving Alex felt somewhat better, but he thought, *We can't survive too many more nights like this.*

After getting the fire going and having breakfast from the supplies that Felix had brought with him, they all felt better.

Felix took Alex and Patricia aside.

"Alex and I will go to the top of the mountain. You stay here with Ayatollah and his daughter, and make sure they don't change their minds about escaping from Iran. I'm going to ask McClelland to go with us, but if he doesn't go, you watch him. We've come too far to blow this deal. You've got your pistol?" Patricia nodded and patted her robe.

Escape from Iran

McClelland decided to go with them, so the three of them went up the mountain together. Even though the day was dreary, walking up the mountain made Alex feel better. It was not a difficult climb. They merely walked up the trail for about a half hour to a spot which overlooked the border.

"Alex, let's stay behind these rocks. We don't want anyone spotting us. It's no good taking unnecessary chances," said Felix.

Down below was the border. It was marked by a swift mountain stream. Alex shivered at the thought of trying to cross it. The water looked icy cold, uninviting and treacherous. The Iranian side was neither marked nor fenced. There was only what appeared to be a trail along the creek bank.

Alex observed, "There are no footprints in the snow, so if the Iranians patrol the border, no patrols have gone by since last night's snowfall."

The Russian border on the far side of the creek was well marked. An area from the creek bank back approximately twenty-five to thirty yards had been cleared. Along the far end of the cleared space was a high fence topped with barbed wire upon which was posted every twenty-five or thirty yards large signs. You could not read the writing from where they were, but Alex surmised it was the usual warning against unauthorized entry. There were no marks in the snow to indicate that the Russians had patrolled the border recently, at least on the creek side of the fence.

Felix, Alex, and McClelland sat for several moments in silence on a rock ledge looking over the river and into Russian territory on the far side.

Felix, who normally volunteered only information essential to the project, broke the silence. He spoke. "During the days before the Shah we used to cross into Russia right down there", he said pointing. "We haven't used it in years, but it still should work. We still have an agent over there. A sleeper. I have already contacted him. Tonight I'll check in by my satellite phone as to whether or not he will be able to meet us tomorrow. Just getting across is not the problem. The big problem is finding a place to hide once we get into Russia. You all will stand out like a sore thumb, and you can't camp out for very long in this weather.

"In the old days this crossing was used fairly often. We had no problem on this side. When the Shah took over, we did not have to worry about using it to put agents into Russia. The Savak, his secret police, and the border police were on our side. They looked the other way.

"If we had an agent on the other side, it was very simple. We shot a line over to him using one of those line-throwing guns like the navy has. And then we would pull the agent across. The Russians were very

Escape from Iran

predictable., their border patrol came through on a timetable like Swiss trains. During the summer months the guards would walk along that path over there between ten and eleven in the morning on Tuesdays and Thursdays. In the winter there would be weeks during which they never came, but if they did come, it was always on a Tuesday morning or Thursday morning. So we knew exactly when it was safe to go back and fourth. My guess is they have not varied that routine since those days."

Alex spoke. "How will we get across this time?"

"The same way. When our agent comes, I'll shoot a rope across to him. He will pull you across. I'll show you."

Later in the morning Alex noticed that Felix continually looked at his watch. The agent had not appeared on the other side of the river. Felix then decided something must have happened to the agent, and that they had better get across on their own.

CHAPTER 49

After a cold lunch Felix produced from under his truck what appeared to be a funny-looking old muzzleloader together with quite a bit of what looked like clothesline. Alex immediately recognized it as part of a breeches buoy, a device commonly used to transfer people and equipment from one ship to another at sea. The problem here was there was no one on the other side of the river to catch the line. Felix attached one end of the line to the gun and put a small grappling hook on the other end of the line. After three attempts the line caught onto some rocks on the far riverbank. "It's too low." Felix said. "I am going to have to swim across and tie it onto a tree higher up the bank."

Bob was watching the procedure with great interest and said, "Felix, the river is too swift and cold you'll die of hyporthermia before you get there."

Felix , ignoring McClelland, said, "Alex, come here and help me. Do as I say. The river is entirely too swift and too cold for all of us to

Escape from Iran

try to swim across it, so old Felix has another solution. It is somewhat clumsy, but it will work In fact. I have used it once before."

Felix and Alex pulled hard on the line across the river, and it held. Picking up a second line, Felix ignored Bob's remark and continued to anchor the line in his hand to a nearby tree, "Alex, you and Bob tie this end of the line around my waist. I'm going to have to wade and swim across. Then I can set up the breeches buoy from the other side. I should be okay, if I can hang onto the line caught on the rock on the other side, and if I keep moving, I don't think I'll get too cold. It's our only chance. The river is too cold and too swift for all of you to try to swim across. Hang onto the rope around my waist. Don't give me too much slack. If the rope I shot across the river doesn't hold, pull me back. As soon as I get across, I'll attach the line to a tree high on the bank so that you all can come across without getting wet. The first one of you to come across please bring me these extra clothes," he said, pointing to a canvas bag lying near by. "I have a jersey and matches in a waterproof container, so I can light a fire, but I'll need warm clothes. I do not want to get pneumonia."

As Felix was completing his explanation of how the device worked, they heard the *wop, wop, wop* of an approaching helicopter. Felix immediately jumped down, shouting, "It's them, Alex run for those bushes and crouch down, and don't look up. A white face will be very visible."

G. Gray Garland

Seconds later an Iranian army helicopter came into view. It was obviously following the border and being careful to stay on the Iranian side of the river.

"Everybody stay down," Felix whispered, as though the occupants of the helicopter could hear him.

The helicopter could no longer be seen, but a faint *wop wop* of its rotor blades could still be heard.

After a few moments Felix looked up. In the distance he could see the helicopter. It had increased its altitude considerably and seemed to be hovering over a distant spot.

"They're too far away to see me in the river. I'll be too low, and at that distance they could hardly see me."

With that Felix waded into the river and started to wade and swim across holding on to the first line so that he would not be swept downriver. He moved very rapidly pulling himself hand over hand on the line, but to the watchers onshore it seemed like it took forever for Felix to get across to the other side. Once there he quickly put on a sweater he took from the bag he carried with him and proceeded to tie the first line high up on a tree so that the others could come across, using the breeches buoy, without getting wet. Within minutes the breeches buoy was up and running.

"Alex, Thank goodness. He's across. Do you think they saw us?" Patricia said..

244

Escape from Iran

"I doubt it. He replied, not believing what he said, "unless they were looking directly at us with a pair of high-powered binoculars. In any event let's just stay here for a few minutes until the helicopter goes on."

Three miles away the army helicopter hovered over a clump of trees as ordered by Lieutenant Hassam.

"Do you think that's them?" asked the pilot.

"I am not sure, the Lieutenant replied, "but they sure as hell look suspicious to me. That is why I did not want you to hover over them. I don't want to spook them. In any event we won't take any chances I'll radio for some help. There should be police or border guards in the area."

CHAPTER 50

Felix had assigned McClelland the duty of monitoring the police radio. He sat in the Toyota staring into space and feeling very sorry for himself. *What will I do, if the Americans throw me into jail. I should never have trusted them. Maybe we won't get out of here, and that could be even worse.*

Suddenly the radio they had taken from the police jeep came alive.

"Headquarters, calling Unit 6."

"Go ahead. This is Unit 6."

"Ahmid, where are you?"

"I'm on the old Qatishx road about 25 miles from Gifan."

"How many men do you have?"

"Corporal Aseri and myself in the jeep and two plus the driver in a weapons carrier following us. Why? What do you want?"

"An army helicopter thinks they've spotted the gang that shot up our road block. Apparently they are some big VIP's who are trying to

246

Escape from Iran

get out of the country. They are hiding on a mountain on the border across from a Russian village. I don't know its name. They want you to go up there and block the road, so they can't get out."

"Why me? What about the border guards?"

"You"re the closest unit. There are no border guard units within fifty miles. For some reason they have been concentrating their search around the regular border crossings. You better get up there as soon as you can. All hell is breaking loose here. It must be a very big deal. I understand the army is moving in to seal the border. And they are sending in a lot of helicopters to patrol it. Do you have your map out?"

"Yes."

Headquarters then proceeded to give the coordinates.

McClelland's heart sank. *Oh God. They know where we are.*

CHAPTER 51

McClelland could hardly believe his ears.

They know where we are, and they are moving in to get us,

Good God, what will we do now.

He broke out in a cold sweat. He sat by the radio for a few minutes stunned. He half listened as orders were relayed to various units, ordering them to proceed immediately to the area where McClelland and his party were.

I'd better tell Felix about this. He may be able to get us across before they get here.

He rushed up the hill to tell Felix and the others only to find Felix had already crossed the river.

Alex listened to McClelland's report, paused for a few moments, and in a calm almost nonchalant voice said, "We've got a real problem here. If we try to cross the river before dark, I'm sure the helicopter will be watching us. We will then be like the proverbial fish in a barrel, only

Escape from Iran

this time we'll be fish in a river. We have got to hope they did not see Felix go across."

The first police unit according to Bob will get here in about an hour to an hour and a half. Since there are only four or five of them, they will likely block the road and do nothing else until reinforcements arrive.

Then, continuing to look at his watch, "I don't see how they can get here until after dark."

He paused again. In the distance the *wop,wop* of a new helicopter could be heard.

"Take cover, and don't look up."

An army helicopter swept by overhead, followed a few moments by a second army helicopter. Neither helicopter paused, so it was impossible to tell whether or not they were seen from the air.

"They didn't seem to be looking for us. They never even slowed down," said Alex.

"Neither would I, if I didn't want you to know, I knew where you were," replied Patricia.

Patricia took her hand and calmly brushed her hair back. "They'll run frequent flyovers, either at a distance or at a high altitude to make sure we have not moved. They have undoubtedly spotted our car and Felix's truck."

Alex spoke, "My guess is that once the police unit arrives, they will block the road and sit tight until reinforcements come, just as you said, but I don't think they will attempt to capture us after dark. It would be too dangerous for them, and besides once they block the road, we are trapped and we can not get out of here."

"I agree, Alex, said Patricia. "Once my reinforcements are in place I would have the helicopters watch the river to prevent a crossing or even land some soldiers there. At that point we're trapped like rats."

"OK, OK, but what are we going to do? I'll tell you what, it was Patricia speaking agian. "If we sit here and do nothing, we have no chance at all. We will be captured. If we try to cross the river in daylight, we will be sitting ducks. The helicopters can hover over us and shoot us like fish in a barrel. Once the first police unit gets here, the road will be blocked, and we can't get our vehicles out of here.

"Here is what I propose. I propose we make a big show of loading up the Toyota. We start down the mountain towards the main road. When we get to a place where we are sure the helicopters can't see us, I'll stop the car for a moment. The Ayatollah, , McClelland and Alex will quickly jump out of the car. Reza will stay with me. I need her because I don't speak Farsi. We'll tie her up, so that she appears to be my prisoner. If we can divert them until dark, you will have a chance of getting the Ayatollah across the river. They'll be looking for us, thinking we are all together and will not be concentrating on this spot. We have

Escape from Iran

the police radio, so we know which way the police are coming. I have a map. I can probably avoid the ground units, at least for a while. If we don't draw them away, we are all done."

"What about the helicopters?" It was Alex speaking. "They'll probably machine gun you."

"I don't think so. They'll figure we can't go anywhere, and sooner or later we will run out of gas, and they'll be able to capture us alive. My guess is, knowing their mentality, they will want to capture us alive and make a big spectacle out of us. If we can keep them running until dark, we'll ditch the car and go cross country. If we can do that, I can probably lose them. I'll come back here and try to cross the river in three or four days."

"That's stupid, Patricia. We can't leave you as the sacrificial lamb", replied Alex.

"Now wait a minute, Alex. I'm a professional agent. I've been trained to take care of myself in situations like this. I'm sure given half a chance I can escape."

"Alex, I think she is right." It was Bob. "Thinking you can get across to the other side without a diversion is wrong. With Felix on the other side he can't help us. If they see us going across, they'll machine gun us."

Patricia intervened, "The important thing is to get the Ayatollah out of Iran. I don't think we have any other choice."

G. Gray Garland

Get the Ayatollah out of here, thought Alex. *What the hell about the rest of us.*

"Bob, explain the situation to Reza and see whether or not she will go with me," said Patricia.

Bob quickly explained the situation to Reza, and she nodded her head in the affirmative.

Patricia said, "That's settled. Okay, gather up your things, and let's get the hell out of here. Take only what you can carry."

"What about the breeches buoy?" said Alex referring to the way which they were going to use to get across the river.

"Leave it. We don't have much time," replied Patricia already going towards the Toyota.

As they all went down the hill toward the Toyota, they could see a helicopter circling in the distance. Felix watched in puzzlement from the other side of the river. There was no way to communicate with him over the roar of the river.

"I'll bet they are watching us through a pair of high powered binoculars", said Bob.

There was no answer. The rest of them were silent.

CHAPTER 52

Lieutenant Leylaz put down the binoculars and thumbed his microphone. "They are moving out."

"Are all of them moving out?" This was Majid's voice.

"Yes Sir. I think so."

"How many did you count?" "I counted five, sir." "Are you sure?"

"Yes sir. I'm sure."

"That's the correct number. It must be them. Keep the vehicle in sight and report to me every few minutes."

"Yes sir. Where are you, sir?"

"I've just left the army air strip at Mashhad. I would guess that I am about seventy-five miles away. Can you talk to the police units on your radio?"

"No sir. I have to relay any communications through the army

base. They call police headquarters by telephone, and then police headquarters radios the police units. I hear that there is one unit on its way up here which should be here in about 40 to 45 minutes."

G. Gray Garland

"Do you know where they are coming from?" "Yes sir," He replied giving Majid the location where the unit was based.

"So they are coming up the main road from the South." Majid looked at the map in his lap and then keyed his mike. "Lieutenant where are they now?"

CHAPTER 53

As they rounded the second curve, Alex practically shouted, "Slow down, Patricia. There is a rock ledge over to the right. It's almost like a cave. Drive under it as closely as you can, and pray."

The Toyota slowed down, and the three men ran under the protective ledge. Alex, who had been prepared to help the Ayatollah, was surprised at how quickly he moved.

They crouched under the ledge and watched the Toyota continue down the mountain and out of sight. It was a lonely depressing sight.

Alex held the walkie-talkie. After what seemed like an eternity, there were two taps. Everyone breathed a sigh of relief. This was the signal that Patricia thought the helicopter was tracking her. Patricia drove down the mountain rapidly She was an excellent driver.

The nearest police unit was coming up from the south and making good time. The other units were quite some distance away and would not arrive for several hours.

G. Gray Garland

Patricia wondered whether she should keep going south. The police unit might be so intent on getting up to their hiding place that it might not notice two women in a Toyota.

Then she heard the police radio. Reza translated. "The police have been told that we are trying to escape south on the main highway. They have been told that there are five of us in a Toyota. They are to take us alive, if possible, but to be careful. We are armed and dangerous.

"Wait a minute. They are changing something." They listened to the radio. After a minute Reza said, "The soldiers have been told to let us through. There are only five of them, and they feel there would be a better chance of taking us alive, if they had more men."

She paused. "They are telling them to follow us with their jeep, try to keep us in sight and to radio our position. The helicopter which has been tracking us had to return for fuel and another helicopter won't be here for another fifteen minutes."

Well, we are having some luck after all, thought Patricia, *They think we are all in the car, and they can track us with the helicopter for a little bit.*

She wished she could tell Alex and the rest of them the good news, but she was too far away to use the walkie-talkie. Then she realized with a sudden twist in her stomach that maybe her luck was not so good after all. She would be caught in a pincer. If she did not go past the

Escape from Iran

roadblock, they would certainly search this area, and if the search was wide enough, they might find Alex and the rest of the party. She had to go through the roadblock and take her chances. She had to draw the searchers away.

CHAPTER 54

"It should be dark in about an hour," said Alex, shivering from both cold and fright.

"I hope Patricia and Reza are all right."

"Well, I would guess by now they are at least twenty miles away, Bob replied. "These walkie-talkies should be good for at least 5-10 miles anyway."

"Or already caught," answered Alex, fingering the transmit button on his walkie-talkie. "You're right. These walkie-talkies probably are not any good for over five miles in these mountains."

That's true, thought Bob, but he did not reply.

"I haven't seen or heard any helicopters for the last hour. They're probably following the Toyota. We've got to go back up the mountain and down the other side to the river. We probably do not have much time. Once they stop that Toyota and find we're not in it they will move up here as fast as they can."

Escape from Iran

"Bob, you start up the mountain now. The Ayatollah will follow you about twenty yards behind. I'll do the same, and I'll bring up the rear. If you see anything give us the old wolf howl, and we will all go to ground.

When we get up to where we camped, we will regroup for a few moments pick up anything we need and head over the hill to the river".

It took about an hour, but they made the camp without incident.

CHAPTER 55

Patricia was on the main road south and moving fast. She was an excellent driver. The Toyota's odometer indicated she had come at least fifteen miles.

The police radio crackled constantly, but not understanding Farsi, she paid little attention to it, except when Reza, who now spoke quite excellent English, would make a comment.

"We should arrive at the police roadblock very shortly," commented Reza.

Patricia was debating whether or not to stop at the police roadblock or to try to run through it. She made up her mind. *If I am going to be a decoy, I might as well be a good one and draw them away as far as I can. If I stop, and they see there are only two of us, they will likely hold us and try to find out where the others are. If I can get through and run, I will certainly buy some time, and if we are very lucky, we might be able to escape.*

Escape from Iran

She turned to Reza. "Fasten your seatbelt tightly. I am going to run the roadblock, if I can. They have orders to take us alive, so I don't think they'll shoot at us."

Reza nodded very grimly.

She is a very brave girl, thought Patricia.

They rounded a bend, and there it was-the roadblock. A jeep and a weapons carrier stood on the road positioned so that an oncoming car would have to slow to a crawl in order to zigzag between them.

Five of the policemen stood behind the jeep with weapons ready.

Patricia decided in a flash. "If I try to go between the cars, I'll have to run down a couple of them, and they will surely open up on us. There is not much room on the berm, but it is worth a chance."

She hit the brakes, slowing down as if she was going to stop for the roadblock, slammed it into four-wheel drive and floored it. The Toyota shot along the berm, wheels spinning, rocks flying.

Patricia braced herself, but no shots were fired.

In the rear view mirror she could see the policeman scurrying for their cars to start the chase. She hated to do it, but she slowed down momentarily to take the Toyota out of four-wheel drive and then roared away.

"We've got to get off of this road before they catch up and see us. Reza, do you know how to read a map?"

"Not very well."

G. Gray Garland

"Okay, well give me the map", she said referring to the map they had used coming north.

"I'm coming to a straight stretch of road. You hold the wheel steady and watch where we are going while I look at the map. Turn on the dome light."

Although she hated to do so, Patricia again slowed the Toyota down to glance at the map and at the road. She handed the map back to Reza and said, "There appears to be a side road about two or three miles from here. It is on the right. Watch for it."

She retrieved the steering wheel and resumed her high speed.

The traffic on the police radio continued to be heavy. One of the police units to the south called to the units pursuing them.

"Do you have them in sight yet?"

"No, but they can't be too far ahead of us."

"Should we continue north or should we stop and set up a roadblock?" replied the unit to the south.

"I think you should stop and set up your roadblock as soon as you find a good place. Be sure you block the sides of the road. They went around our roadblock on the berm. I know you have orders to take them alive, but I would shoot out the tires, the gas tank and the engine, if they don't stop."

"Did you see how many were in the car?"

Escape from Iran

"No, everyone seemed to have ducked down except for the driver."

"Reza, hang on." said Patricia suddenly braking the Toyota and turning sharply to the right. Patricia put the car into four-wheel drive, and they bumped along a trail for 100 yards or so. Then she turned into a field and parked the Toyota behind a clump of bushes.

"Let's go", she said, grabbing an Uzi off the back seat.

"Where are we going?" asked Reza.

"We are going up to the top of this hill. If they find the Toyota, I want to be on the high ground. I can probably hold them off for quite a while. It's getting pretty dark."

They had only gone a few yards when Patricia said, "Shh". They heard the two police vehicles go by at high speed. "Come on, let's go back to the car."

Reza obeyed, and they ran down the hill to the Toyota.

Patricia went to the rear of the vehicle and punched out the tail lights with the barrel of her Uzi.

"I don't want anyone to see us from the rear," she said as they pulled out from the trail and turned north onto the main road. It was dark now and Patricia switched on the headlights.

"About fifteen miles north of here, the road runs along a cliff. I'm going to try to get that far and dump the car over it. No one will find it until daylight, and even then it will take them quite a bit of time to get

G. Gray Garland

down to it. It's a pretty steep cliff, and I don't think there is anywhere down there for a helicopter to land. In any event, it will buy us more time."

The radio crackled again. It was the unit to the south. "We've set up our roadblock in the gorge beyond the bridge over the creek.. The road is narrow here, and we've got it completely blocked."

There was a pause, then the voice on the radio said, "Unit six is just pulling up. Do you have the car you're chasing in sight yet?"

"No, but we are only about five miles from you, so you should see them pretty quickly."

The unit at the roadblock continued, "Two helicopters have just landed. The people you are chasing certainly must be very important."

About a minute later Majid and Lieutenant Leylaz walked from their respective helicopters to the roadblock.

"Well sir, I think we finally have caught them," said the police sergeant manning the roadblock.

Majid merely grunted, "Don't count on it, Sergeant. They are not in custody yet." With that he pulled a Browning automatic from his holster, pulled back the slide, putting a cartridge into the chamber, and returned the gun to the holster. The lieutenant copying his boss this did the same.

"Here they come," said one of the policemen.

Escape from Iran

Lights could be seen entering the gorge. Majid waited a minute or two and then said, "Ok, Captain turn on all of your headlights.

The captain relayed the order. And the headlights of the four vehicles blocking the road came on simultaneously.

Instantly the radio crackled. It was the unit from the North. "We see your lights do you have them? "

Majid's heart sank. He knew again that the fox had eluded the hounds.

CHAPTER 56

Majid paced up and down by his helicopter, talking incessantly to his lieutenant and chain-smoking cigarettes, lighting a new one before he finished the one he was currently smoking, and.

They must have gotten off the road or doubled back. We don't have much chance of finding them tonight. It's too dark. I'll send two ground units north and tell them to look for any signs, but it will be a miracle, if we find them.

"I want you to take your helicopter and follow the main road north. There is a good chance that they may have cut back and are heading for the border. If so, you can easily overtake them. You'll see them from the air. They've got to use their headlights."

"What do I do, if I find them?"

"First, radio me. If you don't see them along the road, I want you to go on up to the border where you first found them. I don't expect you to see anything, but you never know. Remember, if you see them, I can get to you in a few minutes."

Escape from Iran

"I'll stand by here for a while and organize the ground units. They appear to need some organization. If you see them, fly past and block the road. It's the only north-south road. If you can cut them off, they cannot make the border before we can bring up reinforcements and surround them."

"Yes Sir, and. .."

Before he could finish, Majid said, "I would prefer that you would take them alive, but I don't want that car to get through. Shoot out the tires, the gas tank. Do whatever you have to do, but stop that car. Don't let it get past you. And remember, be careful. They shot up a roadblock and killed all the people there."

Moments later the Lieutenant's helicopter, lifted into the sky and headed north.

CHAPTER 57

Patricia was surprised. Reza almost appeared to be enjoying their predicament. For the first time since she had met her, Reza was smiling and lively. In fact, much to Patricia's surprise, Reza had removed her hood and veil. She was quite pretty. As they topped a hill, Patricia looked into the rear view mirror. She could see no one following her.

"Reza, if I remember correctly, we will be coming to a shelf road in a couple of miles. When we get there I'm going to dump the car over the cliff, and we are going to go the rest of the way on foot. Figure out what you need, and when I stop, get it out of here quickly. The patrol coming up behind us can't be too far away, and we don't know whether or not there is a patrol in front of us which may have doubled back to look for us."

Within minutes later Patricia pulled the car off to the side of the road, and she and Reza hastily threw whatever they thought they might need onto the ground.

"Give me that flashlight. Stay here I'm going to dump the car."

Escape from Iran

With that Patricia put the car into gear and drove it across the road to the cliffside. She stopped the car and put on the handbrake. She then took two cardboard boxes and wedged them under the dashboard and against the accelerator so that the engine revved up slightly. She put the car into low gear and eased her foot off the brake pedal. She breathed a small sigh of relief. The handbrake had held.

She then got out of the Toyota and took her flashlight. She shined it along the edge of the road and found the cliff. It overlooked a deep gorge. In the dark you could not see the bottom, and it did not appear that there were any obstructions that would keep the car from going all the way to the bottom.

She reached into the car adjusted the wheels and released the handbrake. The car moved forward slowly at first and then gathered speed as it moved to the edge of the cliff. The front wheels went over the side without any difficulty. The Toyota teetered on the edge of the cliff for a moment and then stopped dead. Its rear wheels came off the ground. The car hung there with the rear wheels spinning in the air. For the first time Patricia felt fear.

"My God, if they find the Toyota there we won't have any chance." She went over to the car and shined her flashlight on it. The front wheels were spinning free above a lip just below the edge of the cliff.

"Reza," she called. "Come here quickly and bring some rope.

G. Gray Garland

"There is no rope. Felix took it all. I hear a car coming," exclaimed Reza.

"We've got time enough. Let's push one more time," said a calm-voiced Patricia.

They both heaved. The Toyota refused to budge from its perch.

"It's not going to work. We've got to run for cover. Let's grab our things and run."

They were just starting up the hill when three pairs of headlights swept around the bend bathing the road in light.

Patricia and Reza scrambled up the mountainside, just as the lead jeep skidded to a stop.

They were near enough to hear the lieutenant in charge shout to his men, "They can't be very far. You two take the jeep and go down the road. Even if they were running, they couldn't get more than a mile. If you don't find them within a mile, turn around and come back. The rest of you get some flashlights and come with me," he said pointing in the direction where the two women were hiding.

"Sergeant, radio headquarters and tell them that we found the Toyota."

The first jeep whizzed on down the road, and the remaining men spread out along the road and began to move toward the mountainside.

Escape from Iran

Patricia and Reza remained frozen. They feared that any movement on their part would give away their hiding place.

The soldiers began to advance, their flashlights beams searching through the darkness. They were about ten to fifteen feet apart as they moved toward the mountainside.

"Lieutenant, we can't go up this cliff at night even with flashlights," said a soldier standing within four feet of where the women were hiding.

The Lieutenant, who had just stumbled himself, replied, "I guess you're right. Okay, men, each of you go up as far as you can, and the rest of you come back to the road. If it's this tough for us, it will be just as tough for them. They can't go very far."

The soldiers, who did not seem to be very enthusiastic about climbing around a rocky mountainside at night, quickly retreated back to the road,

Patricia and Reza each breathed a quiet sigh of relief.

They heard the lieutenant talking on his radio. He was obviously talking to a superior officer.

It was Majid on the other end of the radio transmission. When he heard the news he thumbed his mike and replied, "That's pretty rugged country up there. They can't do too much climbing at night. I can not get any helicopters up there at night. It's too dangerous in that pass, but I'll send reinforcements up at once and hope that we can hold them down until morning."

CHAPTER 58

"It's getting dark now. We'd better try to get across the river before they come for us," said Alex, shivering from both cold and fear. "I will to go to the top of the hill behind us and find a position where I can see the road. If I see anyone coming, I'll come down to us as fast as possible. Bob, you and the ayatollah will go across the river as fast as you can. Since it takes two people to operate the breeches buoy, I don't think you can come back for me. So what I'll do is tie a line on this side of the river and you can take it across with you. When I come across, you will have to pull me over on the line.

"Don't look so startled. I have plenty of extra line. "Come over here. Let me give you this line." Alex moved over next to Bob.

"Bob, I don't know any other way to do this. Obviously we can't leave the ayatollah. I am just a little afraid that he may panic and try to go back claiming that we kidnapped him at gunpoint. Believe me. This will work fine. Just keep your chin up.

Escape from Iran

"Take this flashlight. Make sure the batteries are okay. Take one of the Uzis. I don't think you'll need it, but take it anyway. "We only have the one walkie talkie. Patricia took the other one. So after I go up the hill to see if any of the police are near. If they are not, I'll fire one shot as a signal for you to get across the river as fast as you can. Be careful, it's rocky. Don't rush you'll have plenty of time."

"When you get to the other riverbank, flash your light three times, so that I know you are there. I'll answer with two flashes to let you know everything is all right. When I am ready to come over, I'll flash my light and pull on the rope a couple of times, and you can pull me over."

"Don't worry about bringing anything over with you. We probably don't need any guns over there. Just take the one Uzi and come over as light and fast as you can. I think Felix has a pistol." Alex spoke a few words of encouragement to Bob and to the ayatollah and walked up the hill to watch the road from the other side.

Alex, muttering to himself, *I'm just a sacrificial lamb. To hell with this. If I get out of here alive, I'll never believe the government or anyone, even the president.* He could not remember feeling so frightened and lonely.

It took McClelland, and the Ayatollah about a half hour to cross the river. It was far more difficult in the dark than anyone had anticipated.

273

G. Gray Garland

After Bob and the ayatollah reached the Russian side, Felix took his pistol from his belt and fired it into the air. From his hilltop perch Alex heard the shot with great relief. It seemed like he had been standing watch for an eternity. He started down the slope to the river. Even with a flashlight, it was difficult to move very fast.

Almost at the same instance that Alex reached the riverbank, a helicopter swept around the bend in the river, its search light playing along the Iranian side. Instinctively Alex dived behind a large boulder, hoping he would not be spotted.

They will spot the line across the river that Felix left for me. I've had it.

On the Russian side of the river Felix also saw the helicopter. He held his breath and prayed, "Oh Lord, don't let them see the rope."

The helicopter came on. Its searchlight shined brightly on the line, but the helicopter continued on without slowing. Alex on the Iranian side and Felix on the Russian side simultaneously thought with jubilation, *They didn't see the rope.*

Their spirits were crushed moments later as the helicopter spun around, returned, and hovered over the rope.

Lieutenant Leylaz immediately keyed his mike, "General, I didn't see anything on the road up here, but I think I have spotted the crossing point."

He then proceeded to tell Majid his location.

Escape from Iran

"I can't tell whether or not they got across, but there are two lines across the river. The pilot is afraid to land."

Majid quickly replied," If there are two lines across the river, it probably means someone is still on our side. Otherwise, they would likely pull both lines across, so there would be no evidence of their crossing. When the last one was across they would likely be no lines left. And I'm certain they would cut any lines so that we would not know where they crossed."

Majid paused for a second or two to assess the situation. "Do you see anybody?"

"No, but they could be hiding in some bushes or behind some of the rocks."

"Can you cut the lines? They must have strung them up during daylight. It would be far too difficult to do something like that at night."

Felix, McClelland and the ayatollah, who were now on the Russian side had not been spotted.

"Let me ask the pilot."

There was a pause, and the radio crackled again. "He says he thinks we can get down low enough, so that if I get out on the landing gear, I'll be able to cut it."

There was another pause, then the radio crackled again, "We don't have a knife."

"Well, get the hell down there and shoot it in two."

From the Russian riverbank Felix saw the helicopter slowly descending towards the lines.

"Damn it! They're going to try to cut the lines."

He picked up the Browning automatic pistol he had used to signal Alex that Bob and the ayatollah had made it across the river.

It's a long shot, he thought, *but I've got no choice.*

He braced the pistol on a rock and aimed carefully. He fired twice. The first shot missed its mark, but the second shot knocked out the helicopter's searchlight. The area was plunged into darkness.

The helicopter engine roared and it immediately began to gain altitude.

"I can't see. It's too dangerous without lights," shouted the pilot.

"They just shot out our search light," shouted the Lieutenant into his mike.

"Can you see them?" Majd shouted in turn.

"No not without lights."

"Lieutenant Leylaz was yelling into his microphone, "We can't see anything without our lights, and if we hover too low, they will be able to shoot us down. I only have my service pistol and two extra clips of ammo. We're out gunned."

Escape from Iran

"Get up here as fast as you can. We don't have my helicopter here. It went to get fuel. We'll give you a machine gun. With the machine gun you should be able to cut that rope."

The helicopter rose into the air and disappeared. There was an eerie silence in the gorge.

Alex was stunned. He couldn't believe their good fortune. Several moments passed before he came out of his hiding place under the rock. He looked for the ropes across the river. The lines were still there.

Should he try to get across? He would be a sitting duck, if the helicopter returned. It would take him at least five to ten minutes to get across.

Then he saw a light on the other side alternately jerking up and down in an arc and then flashing four times-the signal that all was clear.

He ran to the bank and listened. There was no sound except for the rushing water. He put on the rope harness that he and Felix had made and jerked the rope twice to start his journey across the rushing icy stream below.

Within seconds Alex was slowly working his way across the river, dangling from the line that McClelland left for him. True, he had a safety line looped over the rope and tied to his body, but he hated heights, and the thought of falling into the roaring river below scared

G. Gray Garland

the living hell out of him, but staying in Iran by himself scared him even more.

It was dark, but he could still see the white foam of the water swirling around the rocks below. And the sound was deafening. It seemed like he was only moving an inch at a time. It was slow work. In spite of the cold he was sweating. He went hand over hand, then hanging on by one hand as he pulled his safety line forward. All he could think of was, *Don't fall, don't fall.*

He finally reached the Russian bank and felt friendly hands helping him down onto the ground. He breathed a sigh of relief, *I'm out of Iran I'm out of that damned Iran.*

Then he remembered. He was not "out of danger". He was in Russia. *Out of the fire into the frying pan.*

CHAPTER 59

The helicopter with its searchlight shattered by Felix's "lucky" shot had not returned, and Alex was safely across the river. For a few moments no one said anything.

Then Felix said, "We've got to get over the fence. We cannot take a chance that someone heard the shots, and a Russian patrol will be sent out.

"There is a place up on the mountainside where we can hide until our agent, Kamenov, comes for us."

Alex and McClelland started for the line across the river. Felix said. "Leave it. There is always a chance that Patricia and Reza may be able to come over tonight while it is still dark."

No one believed that the women would make it across, but no one said any thing.

"Wait a minute," said Felix picking up his bag. "It's a long shot, but we used to have a hole in the fence. It was very well hidden by some bushes. I'm sure the Russians have found it by now and patched the fence, but let me take a quick look anyway.

"Alex, you and McClelland keep your eyes and ears open for any more helicopters while I look for the hole in the fence."

A few moments later Felix called, "I can't believe it, but its still here. Gather up everything and bring it up here."

"What about the lines?" It was Alex.

"Leave them, but bring everything we are taking with us up here, and we will get it through the hole in the fence. Then we'll go back and I'll show you what we will do with the lines."

Within minutes they had taken all of their gear through the hole in the fence.

"Okay, Alex, you stay here with the ayatollah. Bob and I will go and take care of the lines, so they can be used. Watch for helicopters, if you hear or see anything, warn us."

Felix and Bob went down to the riverbank. After they tied the lines to a tree and adjusted the tension so that they could still be used, they rejoined Alex and the ayatollah. Then Felix led them up the steep river bank for several hundred yards. It was steep and the going was rough, but finally after what seemed an eternity Felix said, "We are there."

"There" turned out to be a group of large boulders behind which there was the almost invisible entrance to a cave. The entrance was low and narrow and they had to get down on their stomachs and

Escape from Iran

pull themselves through the narrow opening in order to follow Felix inside.

After crawling ten yards or so, they came to a good-sized chamber in which they could stand up.

"We'll spend the night here, but first we'll light a fire," said Felix, shining his light toward a pile of firewood.

"What about the smoke?" said Alex.

"When our group first located this cave someone lit a cigarette, and we noticed that there was a draft and the smoke quickly dissipated. We then built a fire and were amazed to find there is enough of a draft to take the smoke away. It's no problem at night. During the night the smoke will not be visible, so I think we are pretty safe. Our danger would be someone smelling the smoke, but it is very unlikely that someone would come up the mountainside in the dark at this time of the night.

"Alex, while I get a fire going why don't you go back to the entrance and check to see if anything is going on. Take these binoculars. You'll get a pretty good view of the river where we came across. Take the binoculars and the walkie-talkie. I doubt that Patricia could get back this fast, but you never know."

Alex crawled out to the entrance, wondering what they would do if Patricia and Reza appeared on the opposite bank of the river. He reached the cave entrance in time to see two helicopters sweep up the river their searchlights brightly bathing both sides of the river with light.

Alex watched with sad fascination as one of the helicopters hovered over the two lines, lowered what appeared to be a hook, and cut the lines in two.

He slowly turned and crawled into the cave to report what he had seen. There would be no more crossings of the river tonight.

CHAPTER 60

Patricia and Reza huddled behind their rock on the mountainside. It was cold, and they were both shivering from the low temperature and pure fright. Down below the Iranian soldiers had built a fire on the side of the road, Most of them had gathered around it, seeking its warmth. Most of them were talking and laughing. Three or four soldiers had been posted up and down the road to watch the road and the mountainside.

A second police unit had arrived shortly after the soldiers had retreated back to the road, so there were at least ten or twelve men on the road below their hiding place. Patricia knew that if she and Reza stayed where they were they were certain to be caught. On the other hand, if they moved and were seen or heard, they would likely be caught or shot. From what she had heard of how the Iranians treated prisoners, it would probably be better to be shot. She shuddered at the thought and whispered to Reza, "We can't stay here. As soon as we get a break, we've got to move up the mountain."

CHAPTER 61

That night for the first time in many days they slept well. The fire kept the chamber deliciously warm and cozy. Felix, Alex and McClelland each took their turn at the cave mouth, watching the river below.

The night went quietly.

After having cut the lines across the river the two Iranian helicopters played their lights along the riverbank for a perhaps a half hour or so and then disappeared in the direction from which they had come.

The peace and quiet ended at dawn. Alex was on watch. In the gray light of early morning he could see a great deal of activity on the Iranian side. There were perhaps fifty or more soldiers or policemen searching the riverbank and the rocks along it.

Even if Patricia and Reza had been able to evade the soldiers, there was no way they could cross the river now. Alex felt sick and depressed. They had sacrificed their lives for him.

Escape from Iran

Alex crawled back into the cave to tell Felix and McClelland what had been going on. They were standing by the fire drinking coffee. The ayatollah was still under his covers and appeared to be sleeping.

When Alex relayed what he had seen, Felix said, "It is very unlikely that Patricia and Reza can get across the river today, at least at this place. Here Alex, have a cup of coffee. However, I think we should continue to watch the river just in case they are able to make it to the river and the Iranians have withdrawn their troops.

"Alex, you and McClelland are going to have to take shifts watching the river. One of you must stay with the ayatollah all of the time. The other can stand watch. If the ayatollah wants to go up and watch with you, that's okay too.

"I'm going to leave you for a little bit and go down to the road so that I can watch for Kamenov. By the way, make sure you hide all the guns. If you are caught with guns over here, you are in real trouble. We don't want to be caught with firearms. The Russkies will take a dim view of finding armed Americans on their soil.

"There are plenty of rock ledges along here. Just be sure you hide them in a place where you can find them again. If we have to go back across, we'll need them."

Alex shivered at the thought. *It'll be a cold day in hell, if I ever go back to Iran.* Then it hit him. *It is a cold day, and we are in hell.* With that he headed back to watch the river. Felix disappeared among the boulders and headed up and down the other side of the hill.

CHAPTER 62

Felix had left them to meet Kamenov.

It had turned into a beautiful, sunny day. The air was cold and crisp, but they were quite warm sitting in the behind the rocks, which sheltered them from the icy mountain winds.

The morning was mostly uneventful. Alex, McClelland and the ayatollah sat behind the rocks at the mouth to the cave, mostly dozing in the sun, but occasionally peeking down from their perch to see if there was any activity below. The ayatollah was quiet and somber, obviously concerned about his daughter. McClelland was also silent, apparently thinking about what the future held for him.

They scurried into the cave to hide on only two occasions. First, two Iranian helicopters came down the river, slowly searching the riverbanks. And then later much to their surprise, a large Soviet helicopter came up the river, but it did not appear to be looking for anything in particular.

Escape from Iran

Otherwise, staying out of the cold wind, they dozed in the warmth of the sun.

By noon when Felix returned all was quiet. There were no helicopters to be seen or heard, and the Iranian soldiers had left the opposite riverbank. Apparently they had given up their search.

CHAPTER 63

Felix led them down the other side of the hill to a narrow dirt road where Kamenov and his truck were waiting.

"This is Kamenov. He will take you to a safe place where you can stay until he can arrange your transportation out of Russia," said Felix. "You've got to move out of this area fast. I don't think the Iranians will call the Russkies. It's probably too embarrassing, but we can't take that chance. You don't want to be here if the Russians start searching for you"

"I'll go back to see if there is anything I can do to help Patricia and Reza." Farewells were exchanged, and they drove away leaving Felix standing at the edge of the road and waving goodbye. They all felt a loss. Felix had been their hope and their link, however poor, to survival.

They were pleasantly surprised to find that Kamenov spoke fluent English. He told them he was not really Russian, but an Abidjanian, and he followed this up by saying that all Abidjanians hated the Russians.

Escape from Iran

He said he drove a supply truck, mostly this truck, for a large cooperative and was pretty much able to operate on any schedule that pleased him. This was because of the favors he did for those who were in charge of the cooperative. Cosmetics here, cigarettes there, or other goodies, which he picked up on his trips, went a long way to ensure his independence.

They drove for over four hours on a dirt road and did not pass another vehicle. Alex was amazed and said, "Kamenov, I cannot believe we have not seen any traffic at all."

Kamenov replied, "Well, this is pretty rugged country. There isn't much reason for anyone to come up here, except for the occasional border patrols, and most of them stay around their base drinking and smoking, unless something requires them to go up and check the border. You know, the real answer is they just don't care anymore.

"The Iranians really don't want to come into Russia, and the Russians really don't want to go into Iran. So what's the point of patrolling the border? At least that's their attitude.

"That of course enables us to go back and forth across the border without too much trouble. Sure, we have to be careful of an occasional patrol or a helicopter coming by, but even that's very rare.

"However it's been years since anyone has wanted to come over from Iran. I was surprised to hear from Felix."

G. Gray Garland

"How do you hear from Felix?" asked Alex, holding tightly onto the door to keep from being jolted out of his seat.

Kamenov replied, "I'm not suppose to tell you, but, what the hell, he just calls me on his cell phone."

"You mean he could call you from Iran?"

"No, not exactly. He calls someone, who in turn calls me."

"How did you know the time and place for meeting us?"

"Oh, that was determined by code. For example, if he said 'How is your Mother,' I would answer him with some made up story about her and then proceed to look her name up in a code book, which had been given to you. *Mother* would mean a crossing at such and such a point. It's very simple.

If you were listening to the call, you would have to be a genius to know what is going on. I would say, 'I'll call you after she sees the doctor. What is a good time?' He would then say ten o'clock, and I would know to meet him at the designated crossing point at ten o'clock. Easy and simple, isn't it?

Nowadays people are constantly talking with relatives who are in other countries, especially where they all live near the border, such as that between Russia and Iran. It's impossible to monitor every call, and even if they did, how do you figure out what is meant by innocent sounding talk, such as 'How is Aunt Katrinka'"?

CHAPTER 64

Mike Hogan rushed past Grace Mitchell's desk and into the director's office without being announced. Before a startled Cabot could say, "What is it?" Hogan blurted out, "They've made it. They've made it into Russia."

It took Cabot several seconds to react. His first thought was that he was glad that Blair had gotten out of Iran. This would take him off the hook with the president,the attorney general and Blair's friend in the Senate.. However, on second thought going into Russia could create an international incident, and that would certainly end his career. The problem was not solved by any means. What would he be able to tell the president about this? McClelland was with them. He would claim he was given immunity or pardoned."

Grace Mitchell, who was standing in the doorway and listening to what all the fuss was about said, "Shall I call all of the team back into the office immediately?"

"Yes. And make sure that Robert Gordon is here."

G. Gray Garland

About two and a half-hours later with the exception of Mohammed Azar, the group was assembled in the director's conference room. By this time the Director had more information on what had happened.

"Assistant director Hogan will fill you in on what he knows."

Mike Hogan took over, "Our agent in Iran tells us that Blair, McClelland, and the ayatollah have escaped into Russia, but that the Ayatollah's daughter and our agent, Diaz, were sent back as a decoy and may have been captured. He believes that the Blair group will go north into Russia to go around the Caspian Sea, and then turn to the west and try to escape into Turkey."

Cabot was now all action. He turned to Grace and said, "Get General Harding at the air force on the phone immediately. He's probably not in his office at the Pentagon. Tell whoever answers that it is very urgent that I talk to him at once, no matter where he is."

Turning to Gordon he said, "Robert, I want you to fly to Turkey immediately and handle this matter. We'll relay any additional information to you. Director Hogan thinks he knows where they will cross into Turkey. I want you there when they do."

Grace interrupted Cabot holding up a telephone receiver and waving it at him. "General Harding is on the line."

"Hello, Ralph. Good to hear your voice too. Sorry to disturb you at home. Listen, we have a big problem, and I need the air force's help. I've got to get one of our agents to Turkey as fast as I can...Thanks but

Escape from Iran

wait. I'll also need a plane and some air police to back him up after he gets there. He'll explain it to your base commander in Turkey, and I'll bring you up to date as soon as we can get together. Yes, you are guessing correctly. It is to pick up a very important defector."

Cabot hung up and turned to Gordon. "Get over to Andrews Field as fast as you can. Take my car. Grace will take you down and tell Jerry, the driver, to take you. There is a courier jet scheduled to leave in an hour, but they will hold it up for you. General Harding will instruct our air base at Incirlik to give you whatever you need. He would prefer that any air police working off the base be in civilian clothes. Anyway, you arrange it. General Harding said when you get there report to General Harrington, the base commander. He'll know what to do. You can tell him what we are doing without going into any more detail than you feel absolutely necessary. Don't tell him who you are meeting. I don't want anything to happen to them after they are in our custody. Make sure you coordinate with the Turks. Remember, it's their country. I'll call Turkish intelligence. I'll also arrange with the air force to fly all of you back. Get going and keep us informed."

Gordon rushed out of the office, followed by Grace, whose high heeled shoes were clicking rapidly on the marble floors of the hallway as she was trying to catch up with him.

Within minutes the meeting adjourned, and Cabot returned to his office.

CHAPTER 65

In. the grey light of early morning Patricia and Reza looked down from their chilly perch high on the mountain. Down below them there were several fires going and at least a dozen vehicles clogging the road. During the night more police units had arrived on the scene. However, the soldiers seemed in no hurry to leave the fires and start the search. Perhaps they were waiting for more light, thought Patricia. It was still pretty dark down in the valley. *Or perhaps they are waiting for a helicopter to spot us.*

"Come on Reza, we've got to move again and try to find someplace to hide."

During the night they had literally inched their way up the mountain. Their hands were bruised and bloody, and their clothes were torn and dirty, but they had reached their present site behind some large boulders near the top of the mountain without being discovered. They could not be seen from below, but they were not hidden from the sky.

Escape from Iran

"My guess is that within a few minutes they will have helicopters up here looking for us. We've got to find some cover to get under. Let's get moving."

With that the two tired girls scurried across the small plateau to the other side of the mountain and started down. Patricia prayed they would hear the helicopters in time to find cover to hide under.

Some fifty miles away Majid paced back and forth. It had been light for at least twenty or thirty minutes, and they were still not airborne. He and the pilot and two heavily armed soldiers had come out to the helicopter well before daylight only to discover a pool of oil under it.

Apparently one of Felix's shots had severed an oil line. Two mechanics had been summoned, and after some delay, they were busily repairing the line. But they were still not airborne.

Majid returned to the operations building to see if he could find out anything on the radio.

CHAPTER 66

Patricia and Reza were tired, cold and hungry, but they pushed on. They had no idea where they were going, but they wanted to put as much distance as they could between themselves and the soldiers behind them. It was almost nine o'clock in the morning, and so far they had not heard or seen any sign of their pursuers.

"As soon as we get across that clearing we'll take a rest and I'll try to see where we are on the map."

They had just started across the clearing when it happened.

Two helicopters swooped in fast and low, one hovering directly above them, its prop wash virtually paralyzing them. The other quickly landed nearby. Two men jumped out of the aircraft and ran toward them. One carried an AK47 automatic rifle, which he kept carefully aimed at them. The other was an older man who appeared to be an officer. He had a pistol in his hand.

Patricia and Reza raised their hands. There was no point in offering resistance. In spite of her training Patricia was terrified. She had heard

Escape from Iran

so many horror stories about what the Iranians did to their prisoners. What would they do to an American spy?

The helicopter hovering overhead moved away, and Patricia was quickly disarmed. Within minutes several more helicopters had landed, and there were a number of soldiers and officers milling around them.

Patricia noticed that everyone was extremely differential to the officer who had first captured them. He gave what seemed to be orders in Farsi, which Patricia could not understand. The two girls were handcuffed and separated. Patricia was put into his helicopter, and Reza was put into one of the other helicopters. They immediately took off.

Patricia was very surprised. No one had bothered to question them. All their captors had done was search them and escort them onto the helicopters.

Majid had made his own analysis of the situation. He had been in police and intelligence work for a long time. He correctly deduced that the two girls were decoys, and that the ayatollah, McClelland and Blair had escaped into Russia.

It bothered him a little bit that the lines had been left across the river, but he thought they probably had been left for the two women in hopes they could escape the dragnet and get back to the river. He had received a report on his radio that no one had been found on the Iranian side of the river after a thorough search early that morning

297

by police and soldiers. They had found no one, but they had found evidence that someone had recently been there. One keen-eyed soldier claimed to have seen a man on the opposite riverbank watching them through binoculars, but when his officer in turn trained his binoculars on the spot, there was no evidence of anyone. Majid was now certain in his own mind that the three men had escaped. He was somewhat puzzled that they would leave the two women as decoys, but he felt he would find the answer to that soon enough. He sat beside Patricia in the helicopter brooding. *Should I notify the Russians? If so, I would have to do it immediately. I don't think so. I had better report to the ayatollah. The Ayatollah might consider it a great loss of face to tell the Russians that the Ayatollah Montazeri had escaped. In fact, the Russians are not too fond of the Ayatollah Marzai, and instead of helping, they might use the incident to embarrass him.*

He finally made up his mind that the best thing for him to do was to immediately get in touch with the Ayatollah Marzai and await his instructions. He had better not use the radio. Too many people would hear him and know what was going on.

He motioned to the pilot, "How long will it take us to return to the military airport?"

The pilot answered, "About 12 minutes sir."

Escape from Iran

He turned to soldier in the front seat and said, "When we land I want you to stay with the prisoner until I return. You can remove her handcuffs."

Patricia's handcuffs were holding her arms behind her, and it was very obvious that sitting in the helicopter made her very uncomfortable.

"Shall I put the handcuffs on her front, sir?"

"No, that will not be necessary. She will not try to escape."

Then he turned to Patricia, and in flawless English, he said, "When we land I want you to stay in the helicopter with the guard. Please, no tricks we are landing at a military airport. We have the ability to deal very harshly with those who do not obey our orders."

Patricia, indicating her dirty condition with her hands, replied, "May I please go to the bathroom to wash up?"

Without glancing at Patricia, Majid said to the guard, "Okay, take her to the bathroom and then bring her back here to the helicopter. Make sure the bathroom has no rear door or window. If she tries to escape, shoot her, but don't kill her. I want to question her after I report to the ayatollah."

Majid, still brooding about not being able to stop the escape of the Ayatollah Montazeri repeated his instructions to the guard, "Okay , take her into the restroom, but keep your eyes on her. If she tries anything, put the handcuffs on her. When she is done, meet me by the door to the commanding officer's office. Don't be too long. I have a phone call to make. As soon as I do that, Ill be ready to leave. I want to get back to Tehran as fast as I can. "

Without so much as a glance at Patricia or the soldier guarding her, Majid left the helicopter and strode into the airport office building. He found the commanding officer's office and immediately placed a call to the Ayatollahh Marzai in Quom. The line was busy .

He redialed the number several times. The line was still busy. He redialed several more times. The line continued to be busy. He tried to place a call to his office in Tehran. There was only a busy signal. Apparently all the circuits were busy .

After about twenty minutes, he was able to get through to the ayatollah's office in Quom He reported what had happened to the Ayatollahh Homain, who took the phone call.

"The Iman will be very disappointed. I'm sure, General, that you did your best. We'll determine whether or not to notify the Russians. Bring the women back to Tehran. We can probably get some mileage out of the American woman, and who knows, we might induce the Ayatollah Montazeri to return when he learns what will happen to his daughter, should he not return. And General, as soon as you return, I'm sure the Ayatollah Marzai would like to see you here."

With that the line went dead.

Majid was relieved and at the same time very let down. Would they punish him for something over which he had no control? In fact,

Escape from Iran

it was he who had advised them not to permit the Americans to come to Iran.

With that he left the office to determine whether the helicopter carrying the Ayatollahh's daughter had landed. As he entered the lobby, he spotted Patricia walking toward him with her guard trailing a few paces behind her. He stopped and stared. Her beauty was startling. He had never really noticed her before. When she had been captured her face had been smeared with dirt, and her hair had been unkempt.

Now he could not keep his eyes off of her.

He suddenly felt weak in his knees. His heart began to race. "I must be going out of my mind," he thought. "The pressure is getting to me."

It was not Patricia he was seeing. It was Susan.

CHAPTER 67

Majid quickly got a grip on himself.

Patricia noticed his startled expression and how suddenly his face had paled. She instinctively said, Are you all right?"

"Yes. Yes I'm fine."

"Sergeant, I want to question the prisoner alone in the Base Commander's office. I want you to stand guard, and I don't want to be disturbed by anyone. Do you understand?"

"Yes sir."

With that he ushered Patricia into the office and closed the door behind him. He still was pale and a little shaken.

Patricia again said, "Are you sure you are all right?"

He replied, "Yes. Yes, I'm fine. It was just that you reminded me of someone I used to know."

"My mother," Patricia replied, "You are Majid. "

"How, how did you know?"

Escape from Iran

"1 guessed," replied Patricia. "My mother has spoken of you often. You were her good friend when you attended Harvard, and she was at Radcliff. She has often spoken fondly of you and wondered what happened to you. She wondered why she never heard from you."

Still stunned, Majid said, "How. how is your mother? "

She is fine." Patricia was at a loss for words, but she said, "Do you have a family?"

He replied, "No, I never married." He thought, *I've waited all these years in bitterness to get even, but now that I have the opportunity, I can't do it. This girl could have been my daughter. I can't do it. Allah, I've got to save her. Help me!*

He said quietly, "Patricia, I am going to try to help you. I shouldn't do it, but I'm going to try anyway. But first tell me something. McClelland, the Ayatollah Montazeri and Blair crossed the river into Russia didn't they?"

Patricia decided she had nothing to lose by telling the truth. In fact, if they had not crossed into Russia, and she said they had, the manhunt would probably be called off. "

"Yes they have."

"Then you and Reza were decoys?"

"Yes, the important thing was to get the ayatollah out of Iran. Blair had no experience in this sort of thing, and he did not speak Farsi. We

G. Gray Garland

did not want to use McClelland, so that left me. I did not speak Farsi, so Reza volunteered to come with me."

Majid did not ask if they received any outside help, and Patricia did not volunteer that Felix had been with them.

"Just as I thought," said Majid.

There was a knock on the door.

"Sir, the helicopter with the Ayatollah's daughter is awaiting your instructions. Do you want us to bring her in? Your jet is also here."

"No, put her on my plane and hold her there. We will be leaving for Tehran in a few moments. Send my pilot in." Majid waited until the door was closed and said," Do you know how to use a pistol?"

"Yes I do."

He pulled up his pant leg and pulled a small automatic from a holster attached to his leg just above his ankle.

"Take this. It's an old trick I learned when I was in the States. Most policeman carry a second backup gun. In the States it's usually unregistered so that if they get in a jam for shooting someone, they can claim he had the gun.

"In any event I'm going to send you back to Tehran on my jet. There will be only you, Reza, the guard, and the two pilots. As soon as you are airborne disarm the guard and have Reza put his handcuffs on him. Take his gun and cover the co-pilot. The pilots are usually not armed, but make sure the co-pilot has no weapon. Don't worry about

304

Escape from Iran

the pilot I'm going to have to tell him what we are doing. He is one of my men, and we can trust him. Order the pilots at gunpoint to fly you to Turkey.

"Don't let anyone use the radio. I don't think you will have any trouble with Turkish fighter planes, since they probably won't scramble for just one plane.

"I'm going to tell the pilot to ask you where you got the gun. Tell him you found it by the toilet in the airport when you went to wash up. He'll say I don't believe you, and you can say you really don't care, because it's the truth. You are getting out of Iran, so what difference does it make to you? In any event the guard and the co- pilot will hear it, and hopefully…" His voice trailed off."

Also," he hesitated, "please when you get back to the states give my love to your mother, but be very careful what you say. My life will be on the line, if anyone finds out what I've done."

Patricia was too stunned to speak. She was about to reach for his hand to thank him when he called guard.

The door opened. "Yes sir."

"Take the two girls out to my plane. You will accompany them back to Tehran and turn them over to Major Hassam. I'll arrange for him to meet you at the airport. This American she-devil tells me the others escaped into Russia, but I don't believe her. I think we cut the line before they got across.

"In any event, I'm going to take the helicopters back to search the area again. I don't want to take a chance that they are still here. Do you understand?"

"Yes sir."

"That will be all."

He spotted his pilot entering the lobby. "Captain, come here please."

CHAPTER 68

As Majid strolled out to his helicopter he watched the Jet with Patricia and Reza come booming down the runway and lift into the sky. His thoughts were almost spinning out of control. *I have committed treason. What will happen to me? Will I escape being punished? I never wanted the American to come here. I even tried to have him killed before he came. Did I do the right thing? I don't know.*

Majid fastened his seat belt and directed the pilot to return to the border crossing where they had cut the lines. "I don't believe they all got across. Otherwise they wouldn't have revealed their position and shot at the first helicopter," he lied. hoping he sounded truthful.

He noticed a small bag on the seat next to him. *It must have been Patricia's, he thought.*

He opened it. Nothing, but tissues of Kleenex and two Snickers candy bars. *I haven't had a candy bar since I was in the States.*

He ravenously peeled off the wrapper of one of the bars and chewed it with abandon.

CHAPTER 69

They drove all day, mostly going north, always staying on back roads and stopping only long enough to relieve themselves or to take enough time for Kamenov to fill the gas tank from several large gas drums he had in the back of the truck. They never stopped where there were people or at any of the few places they passed that sold gasoline. Kamenov had a supply of sandwiches and a large thermos of coffee. The sandwiches were slightly stale and the coffee tasted bitter to Alex, but everyone, including Alex, ate and drank with gusto. Alex was surprised to notice that the coffee jug had been made in the USA. They consumed the coffee and sandwiches as they drove, quite often spilling the coffee as the truck went over ruts on the back roads.

The cab of the truck was cramped with all four of them jammed in it, but it was at least warm. After being cold for so long, they all relished the warmth of the truck's heater. For the first time in what seemed like ages, they were not cold.

Escape from Iran

When Alex asked Kamenov where they were heading, he replied that he did not know. His instructions were to deliver them to another agent who would carry them on the next leg of their journey.

At dusk they pulled into a farmyard. Kamenov said, "This is where you'll spend the night."

It was a delicious night. For the first time in days, Alex was able to take a hot bath. He was also able to wash his clothes and sleep in a comfortable bed. Even the ayatollah and McClelland seemed more relaxed.

However, they were both quiet with their own thoughts-the Ayatollah worrying about Reza and McClelland about his future if and when they reached the States.

When they awakened the next morning, Kamenov was gone. In his place with a similar truck was a man. who introduced himself to them as Iben Orpov.

For several days they continued to travel north. Alex could tell their direction by the position of the sun. They stopped each night at an isolated farmhouse or slept in the truck. Each day a new driver took over. He would usually meet them at their overnight stop. After introducing their new driver, the old one would say goodbye and leave them. They apparently did not want the trucks to stray too far from their home territory and possibly be noticed by the authorities.

309

G. Gray Garland

Then they turned west and repeated the process for several more days.

Alex surmised that they were heading west to Turkey. He guessed that they had gone north of the Caspian Sea before turning west toward Turkey. He asked the current driver, who spoke some English, "Are we heading for Turkey?"

"I think so," was the reply in broken English.

"How will we get across the border? It must be guarded very tightly," said Alex.

"I don't know," said the driver. "I've never been that far west."

When Alex was not dozing from the warmth and motion of the truck, he was intrigued by the scenery. The roads over which they traveled were mostly dirt, and they passed very few vehicles. Obviously they were not taking a direct route or using the better roads. They stopped for gas only once at a very primitive gas station where the driver seemed to know the proprietor. Usually they had filled the tanks of the trucks from a supply of jerricans that they each carried.

During the entire trip they saw no police or military personnel.

After several days of travel their present driver told them that they were approaching the Russian Turkish border.

The trip had been uneventful. Although Alex and the rest of them were somewhat apprehensive about being arrested in Russia, they were

Escape from Iran

sufficiently tired from their time in Iran that they continued to doze during much of the trip.

Zig Karpoff to whom they had been turned over at the last stop told them, "Tonight you will cross into Turkey."

"How will we do it?" asked Alex, shuddering at his memory of the crossing into Russia from Iran.

"You'll see," was the reply.

CHAPTER 70

In late afternoon on the fourth day after leaving their hiding place in the cave by the river, they reached the outskirts of Yerevan on the Russian-Turkish border very late at night.

Their driver said to them," That old building ahead of us is as far as I go. The city limits are about two kilometers ahead. The Russian police patrol to that point, and if they see a strange truck, they might stop us. I can't take that chance.

"Walk singly and stay about fifty to seventy-five yards apart. Stay in the shadows and walk briskly. If you see any cars coming, get into the shadows and hide, if you can find a place to hide. The chances are that you'll have no problem, but if one of you is picked up, the others should stay in hiding until the police leave. Go six blocks, and you'll come to a wide street on your right, which dead ends at this street. Just beyond the intersection you will see a taxi. You can tell it's the correct taxi by the bent fender on the driver's side.. You can tell it's your taxi

Escape from Iran

by the driver's cap, which says 'Pittsburgh Steelers'. He will take you to where you will stay tonight.

"Oh, leave your luggage here. I will see that it is delivered to you. You will look less suspicious, if you do not have luggage."

The truck stopped, let them out, made a U-turn, and disappeared in the direction from which they had come. For a moment or two they stood lonely and silent. There was a certain sense of security that they all felt being in the custody of their driver.

Alex broke the silence, "We'd better get going. Bob, you go first. The ayatollah will follow and I'll bring up the rear. It's getting so damned dark, I don't think we'll have to stay as far apart as fifty yards. Let's try to keep in sight of one another. If we see anyone, get into the shadows, and wait until they are well out of the way, but don't look like you are afraid to be seen."

The street was dark and deserted. They passed only one house with a light on. Through the window they could see someone hunched over a table eating or writing-they could not tell which.

They arrived at the corner without incident and much to their relief the taxi was waiting. Just as they had been told, the driver wore a cap, which said "Pittsburgh Steelers". They were relieved to find that he spoke English.

Once they had all settled in the taxi Alex asked, "Where did you get that cap?"

313

"My brother sent it to me."

"Your brother?"

"Yes, he lives in Pittsburgh."

Surprised Alex asked, "How did he get there? I thought it was very difficult to get exit visas?"

"About two years ago our government announced that they would permit a number of Jews to leave the country, so he applied and was accepted."

"Then you are Jewish?"

"No, we are not Jewish. We've never been Jewish. My cousin who is a high party official was in charge of the immigration program from this area, and he slipped my brother in. No one really knew the difference. My brother worked on a farm outside of the city. He just disappeared, and there was no real effort to find him. I shouldn't tell you this, but I thought maybe once you get out of here you might be able to help me to go to the United States.

"I would not have too much trouble getting over the border into Turkey, but the Turks are really tough. If I don't have money and a sponsor in the United States or some other country, they'll ship me right back here, and I'll spend the rest of my life at hard labor in prison or worse.

"However, if I had a influential sponsor, such as you, I'm sure the Turks would let me go onto the United States. My brother works in an

Escape from Iran

automobile body shop in Pittsburgh, and he says if I come over he is certain he can get me a job there."

Alex somewhat taken aback, mumbled, "If you can send me information after we get over into Turkey, I'll see what I can do. I can't promise anything, but I will look into it. "

They did not cross the border that night. No explanation was given.

Instead the taxi drove them to a safehouse and turned them over to another agent, Boris Yesenko. For three days they were not allowed to leave the safe house. They were not even allowed to look out of the windows during daylight hours. The house was warm and comfortable, especially after living outside in the cold. Alex thought the food was awful, but it was better than nothing.

What really bothered him was being so close to freedom and yet so far away.

Their hosts were a middle-aged couple. Only the husband spoke English, and it was very broken English. It was obvious that he did not know anything about what was going on. He was unable to answer any questions. He always said, "Don't ask me. Ask Boris."

Alex concluded that he really did not know and was likely hiding the three of them for extra money or scarce goods. However, their host was careful that they obeyed the rules laid down by Boris, and he watched their every move.

G. Gray Garland

Every day Boris Yesenko, who was apparently in charge of their stay, visited them. Although he dressed like a poor worker, he spoke perfect English and was very self-assured, even cocky at times. He appeared to know everything, but when he was asked, and he was asked at least once or twice each day, when they would cross over into Turkey, he always replied in a somewhat condescending manner, "Don't be so impatient. I'll let you know when I think it is the proper time."

He was very clipped in his conversations. He said only what he deemed was necessary and nothing more. He never elaborated. Alex, McClelland and the ayatollah were obviously to be told "only what he thought they needed to know."

At night they could look out of their window and see the lights of buildings in Turkey across the River.

Alex and McClelland spent many hours talking of the old days and old friends. McClelland would look at the lights and say, "Just think, tomorrow I will be a freeman, living in my own country with my own people."

Finally after three long days Boris announced that they would cross into Turkey that night. "Actually you'll be going across about four o'clock in the morning."

"How will we cross?" asked Alex

Escape from Iran

"I'll take you down to the bridge, and you'll walk across. Don't be nervous. We've been waiting here until the right bridge guards were on duty.

You see, two of the guards cooperate with us. The two are only on duty together about every thirty days. There is a fairly large contingent for the bridge. The Russians rotate the guards. They believe this keeps them honest. You are lucky that we only had to wait three days. The bridge crossing is closed every night at midnight. No one is allowed to cross. A pole is lowered across the roadway to keep any vehicles from crossing, and only two guards are on duty at night to prevent anyone from crossing on foot. During the day there are more guards, but at night with no traffic there are only the two.

"I'll drive you to the bridge, and you will walk across. Don't take any luggage. We'll get it to you later. In my truck will be some tools, a shovel, a crowbar, etc. You will pick them up and carry them across. If anyone does see you, they will think you are workers doing some emergency repairs to the bridge before the morning traffic commences.

"It should be as you Americans say, "A piece of cake.""

True to what Boris had told them, he drove them in a battered dump truck to the bridge. They picked up tools from the truck bed and began to walk across.

It was damp and foggy. It reminded Alex of an old black and white spy movie.

The guards, obviously knowing what was happening, stayed out of the way. The group never saw them. Nevertheless, they felt naked and vulnerable under the lights that lit the Russian end of the bridge. However, they ducked under the pole and went across without any hindrance.

The Ayatollah Montazeri and McClelland followed by Alex walked across the bridge and through the gate into Turkey. McClelland turned to Alex and with a sigh said, "I never thought I would make it. At last I am a free man. My tomorrow has finally come."

As they came off the bridge into Turkey, they could see at least a dozen men standing in the shadows. One moved towards them and a familiar voice said, "Welcome home Alex. You did good." It was Robert Gordon

A shot rang out. It was very a loud and sharp in the damp air.

Everyone ducked.

Alex turned to McClelland to reply. McClelland had fallen on his knees and was slumping onto the wet pavement. Alex fell on his knees and rolled McClelland onto his side. He could see blood. McClelland whispered, "Help me. I think I have been shot. I am not going to make it."

Within what seemed like seconds Turkish border patrolmen and a number of other men, whom Alex assumed were Robert Gordon's CIA men, surrounded Alex and McClelland.

Escape from Iran

One of Robert's men knelt down by McClelland and placed his hand on McClelland's neck. He looked up at Robert Gordon and shook his head. "He's dead."

Alex took McClelland's lifeless body in his arms and crying softly whispered, "Oh God. Your tomorrow never came. What have I done?"

Robert and one of the agents gently picked up Alex, and several of Gordon's men quickly grabbed him and propelled him into a waiting car. With its back wheels spinning the car immediately roared away. It had all happened so quickly that Alex was in a daze.

CHAPTER 71

Alex was thrown back as the car lunged forward and picked up speed. He wondered, *Why was McClelland shot? Who could have done this? Did the Iranians do this to punish him for helping to get the Ayatollah out of Iran? I wonder? No, I think the Iranians would more likely kill the Ayatollah.* Suddenly Alex had a thought and started to sweat. *Would the Americans kill McClelland? The instant they had stepped off of the bridge security was very heavy. There must have been at least twenty people, who were in the shadows. Many were in uniform, some carrying automatic weapons slung over their shoulders. Also there were a number in plain clothes. It would be difficult for an Iranian assassin to be there. Besides, how would the Iranians know when and where they were crossing into Turkey?*

As soon as McClelland had been pronounced dead, Alex had been quickly ushered by Robert Gordon's men into a car that was waiting behind a building at the end of the bridge. Their car, a large Mercedes sedan, that Alex believed was probably armor plated beause of its heavy

320

Escape from Iran

ride, had roared away followed by several escorting vehicles. After a short time they stopped at a hotel.

Robert Gordon, who appeared from one of the other vehicles, said "We're going to have to stay here overnight. The airport is fogged in. It's supposed to lift in an hour or so, but we'll wait until morning. I don't want to take any chances with the ayatollah now that we have gotten him this far.

This hotel here isn't the Plaza, but it will probably seem pretty luxurious after where you've been."

Robert did not ask about Patricia or Reza. Alex assumed he must have heard from Felix.

When they reached the hotel, the ayatollah , who had been in one of the other cars, was quickly escorted away by Robert. He disappeared into the elevator surrounded by at least five or six security people.

The hotel was not all that bad. It was a very old building. The lobby was filled with very ancient overstuffed furniture, which appeared to be in need of reupholstering, fake potted plants in brass urns and even a number of spittoons. As in many European cities, it was called "The Metropole". However, it was clean, and the lobby was filled with what were obviously security people. However, to Alex it seemed like the finest hotel in the world. He was at last free. He never thought he would make it.

321

G. Gray Garland

Robert appeared briefly and handed Alex a Beretta pistol. "I don't think you'll need it, but keep it handy just in case. I'll see you in the morning." With that Robert disappeared wending his way through the mass of security people.

Even though it was very late the reception desk was open. Alex was able to purchase a razor, a toothbrush and toothpaste.

He noticed a newspaper on the counter had a large picture of the Ayatollah Marzai under huge black headlines. It was apparently in Turkish. He asked the girl behind the counter what the headlines meant.

She replied in perfect English, "The Ayatollah Marzai is dead."

As soon as Alex was alone in his room, he placed a call to Elizabeth in Florida. The telephone instrument was old, but much to his surprise the call went through immediately. "Elizabeth…"

"Oh Alex," Elizabeth's voice answered with very obvious relief and happiness. "Are you all right? Where are you? What took so long? Everyone is worried about you. I've so many things to tell you. It's all been so strange. Once or twice a week a postman comes to the Atwood's house with a registered mail letter for me to sign for, but while I'm signing for a blank letter, all he says is that I'm not to tell anyone that you have been heard from, and that you are safe and all right. And the Atwoods say they have never seen so many police cars patrolling the neighborhood since they moved here.

322

Escape from Iran

"Oh Alex, what in the world is going on? Are you in some kind of trouble?"

Alex didn't answer. He couldn't get a word in edgewise. Finally Elizabeth calmed down.

"I'm fine. I'm in Turkey. We'll probably leave for the United States tomorrow or the next day. I can't say much more now. I can hardly wait to get home."

"Have you heard anything about my deal to buy the PC&R?"

"Mike Woodley called to ask if I had heard from you. He said the Government has approved it. According to him the approval was perfunctory, but for some reason the Federal Trade Commission had held up granting the permits or whatever they give you. He's very puzzled. Such a delay has never happened before, and he could not seem to get a straight answer. However, everything is okay now. They're all waiting for you and wondering where you are."

"Well, maybe the Government hasn't forgotten me after all," replied Alex rather sarcastically. "Just tell them I'll be home in a couple of days. Don't tell them anything else. I'll explain the whole thing when I get home."

Elizabeth, now that she knew Alex was safe, as usual, interrupted and continued. "The big news in Richmond is about Betsy Slot."

"Who is she?"

G. Gray Garland

"Oh, you know her. She belongs to Fox Meadow Club and lives up the street from us."

"I still don't know her," said Alex wondering, *What's so important about someone we really didn't know.*

"You know her. They sometimes call her "Betsy Slut", the girl with the open-door policy.' Well, anyway she was badly burned in a fire at a motel."

"So what's important to us about that?"

"A motel in Richmond, but guess who was with her?"

"Come on, Elizabeth. How would I know."

"It was Michael Ralph, our postman."

Alex depressed by this, thought, *I'm home! Back to the real world and the important things in life.*

After a few more minutes of this "important" conversation, he hung up the telephone and stretched out on the bed. He was happy to be out of Iran and Russia, but strangely distressed. It was a feeling he could not understand.

There was a knock on the door to his hotel room. "Who can that be at this hour?" he thought. He pulled out the pistol Robert Gordon had given him, cocked it, and putting his foot in a position to block the door, he carefully cracked it open.

"Hello stranger!" It was Patricia.

Epilogue.

When Majid returned to his helicopter he noticed several Snicker bars, which had been left by Patricia when she was captured. He ate one.

Within a week of Alex's return to the United States the PC&R deal was consummated, and Alex became chairman and chief executive officer of one of the largest conglomerates in the United States.

Patricia Diaz resigned from the CIA. Soon after the Iranian adventure she married a wealthy lawyer from the Washington, DC area. They purchased a farm near Middleburg Virginia, where Patricia raises horses and children. She now has five children, three boys and two girls and frequently visits her family, wherever they may be, especially in Argentina and Spain.

Alex and Patricia and their families have kept in touch over the years.

Printed in the United States
219534BV00001BA/1/P